W9-CBE-302

blue
rider
press

THE SHAPE OF THE FINAL DOG

AND OTHER STORIES

BLUE RIDER PRESS   *a member of Penguin Group (USA) Inc.   New York*

THE SHAPE OF THE FINAL DOG

AND OTHER STORIES

HAMPTON FANCHER

blue
rider
press

Published by the Penguin Group
Penguin Group (USA) Inc., 375 Hudson Street, New York, New York 10014,
USA • Penguin Group (Canada), 90 Eglinton Avenue East, Suite 700,
Toronto, Ontario M4P 2Y3, Canada (a division of Pearson Penguin Canada
Inc.) • Penguin Books Ltd, 80 Strand, London WC2R 0RL, England •
Penguin Ireland, 25 St Stephen's Green, Dublin 2, Ireland (a division of
Penguin Books Ltd) • Penguin Group (Australia), 250 Camberwell Road,
Camberwell, Victoria 3124, Australia (a division of Pearson Australia Group
Pty Ltd) • Penguin Books India Pvt Ltd, 11 Community Centre, Panchsheel
Park, New Delhi–110 017, India • Penguin Group (NZ), 67 Apollo Drive,
Rosedale, North Shore 0632, New Zealand (a division of Pearson New
Zealand Ltd) • Penguin Books (South Africa) (Pty) Ltd, 24 Sturdee Avenue,
Rosebank, Johannesburg 2196, South Africa

Penguin Books Ltd, Registered Offices:
80 Strand, London WC2R 0RL, England

Library of Congress Cataloging-in-Publication Data

Fancher, Hampton.
    The shape of the final dog and other stories / Hampton Francher.
        p.   cm.
ISBN 978-0-399-15823-0
I. Title.
PS3606.A53S53   2012   2012018178
813'.6—dc23

Printed in the United States of America
10 9 8 7 6 5 4 3 2 1

BOOK DESIGN BY NICOLE LAROCHE

ALWAYS LEARNING   PEARSON

FOR MANON

CONTENTS

THE SHAPE OF THE FINAL DOG

AND OTHER STORIES

THE BLACK WEASEL

seen him three times before he attached himself to me. Walking down the street on my way to work was time number one. He caught my attention because of how he was walking, like he was on drugs or something. Plus the suit—you could tell it was a rich guy's suit, like a banker would wear, but it was dirty, like he'd been sleeping in alleys. Got a tie on even, but the thing was, he wasn't wearing any shoes. So I thought, Christ, here's some well-to-do Negro who must have gone mad, got his shoes stolen.

Then what he does is step out into the street, not looking where he's going, and almost gets creamed by one of those big tourist buses. The driver gives him a blast of the horn, he stumbles backwards and starts running away.

That was the first time. I was on my way to work, like I said. The Torture Chamber. It's a nightclub, all of it made to look like some kind of dungeon. You pay twenty-five bucks to get in, dinner and drinks are extra. Al, the owner, gets the entertainment cheap. There's not a big demand for the kind of kinky stuff these people do. He makes all the money, and what they get is free chicken dinners and minimum wage for hanging by chains from their appendages with needles sticking out of their bodies. Big Al had the idea that pain was here to stay, so why not take advantage of it?

It's a specialty club, a regular stop on the tourist circuit. Mainly Japs and people from Europe. The faggots in the show have to be careful, though, say some drunk foreigner gets inspired and tries to get involved. But Big Al's got bouncers, big mean guys in black tights wearing leather masks. You get out of line and see one of these guys coming at you, you'll go and sit back down again.

I walk into Big Al's office. He's sitting behind his desk with his back to me. I stand there with his dinner, waiting for him to turn around. He doesn't.

My mother died, I tell him.

So did mine, he says.

I mean last night.

Sorry to hear it, he says, and keeps watching the monitors. The one that shows the street out front is showing a bunch of Germans piling out of a tour bus like the one that almost hit the Negro.

Big Al's big on surveillance, got cameras all over the place. Outside, inside, even downstairs in the men's room, a camera covering the wash-up area. He'd have one in the crapper if it wasn't against the law. He's waiting for me to put down the tray, but I don't. On the desk, Spence. He spells it out: D-E-S-K. I put the tray on the desk.

Fucking Germans, he says. Tells me I'd better get downstairs. What's the rush, I felt like saying, but I just stood there waiting for him to swing around so I could tell him what I'd been waiting to say. But it was the wrong time. The Germans screwed it up.

So he sits there watching the monitors, making me wait, showing me how important he is. The girls who work for him hate his guts, and he's walking around with his big mustache, his Italian muscles, thinking he's king shit. And I'm still being punished for a gamble I took. What I did was took some piddly amount of money from the till, got caught, got punished, paid the price. He likes people to call him Big Al, but not me, I won't do it. I just call him Al.

Al, I'd like to work upstairs again.

When you're ready, he says.

I am, I'm ready, Al.

You're on probation. Go back down there and do your job.

I'm a bartender, Al.

You *were* a bartender, and would be still if you weren't a fuckin' thief. Now get back down there before I brain you.

I'm fed up with treating him right, but if I didn't, I'd go to jail. He'd tell the cops what I did, and before they'd take me away, he says he'd brain me with a baseball bat. He's got one too, keeps it under his desk.

Being a bathroom attendant isn't exactly what I came to New York City to do. People come down drunk, piss all over the place, vomit maybe. But it isn't just about keeping things clean. The show upstairs could inspire perverts to come down, try and suck each other off. If I catch somebody doing something shady, my job is to put a stop to it. If they don't cooperate, I call one of the bouncers. So I'm sort of a guard too. For this I get a living wage plus whatever they leave in the bowl. I don't mean the toilet bowl. It's a dish I keep on the sink for tips. I stock it with a few bucks to give 'em the idea, but at the end of the night, usually it doesn't amount to much.

Basically Big Al was taking advantage of me, had me over a barrel. I had to wear a white coat too, like the ones the busboys wear. At first I thought, okay, I'll sit it out. But after a while it was pretty clear, this had to be the most boring job in the universe, unless you like to kiss ass, which at first I tried, handing out a towel or sweeping off their shoulders with a little whisk broom. But not unless they're drunk do they want anything to do with you, and if they're not drunk, they pretend you're not there.

Drunk Germans, four of 'em. They barge in yelling, knocking into each other, not noticing me at first. Then one of 'em sees me, looks right at me, making it clear he thinks something's funny. His buddies giggling at

HAMPTON FANCHER

whatever it is he's saying. I'm tempted to say something myself, but it's four against one, so I stay on my stool. The first one, after he pisses, makes a big show out of dropping coins, one after the other, into my bowl, and out they go, charging up the stairs, laughing. I take a look. The coins aren't even American. Big joke. Sometimes I get so bored, the only thing I can do is do a good job—get down on my hands and knees with the gloves on and make everything shine.

On my way home I'm still thinking about those Germans. It's close to dawn. I walk over a grating, then back up to see if what I thought I saw I'd seen. It's the Negro, the one who almost got hit by the bus. He's laying about a foot under the sidewalk. How he got down there, I don't know. Grating must have been loose, he yanked it off, I suppose, got in there, then put it back. A stupid place to spend the night, people walking on top of you, spitting, dropping their butts. He was squinting up at me like he'd found a good place to hide. It was none of my business. I walked on. That was time number two.

I went home, went to bed, but couldn't sleep. Sometimes I do, sometimes I don't. The trucks, the honking, all that stuff. So sometimes what I do is say "Auto" over and over again. Not auto, like car. That's not what it means. Auto is the name of my mother's mule down in Townsville, Mississippi. Auto goes to sleep anytime he feels like it, wherever he happens to be. Just stands there and—bang—he's asleep if he wants. So on bad nights I concentrate on the mule, make a picture of him in my mind, and keep saying his name. And it worked that night; reason I know it did is because I had a dream.

It was me walking down an alley high up over my hometown, which is a dream for sure because my hometown doesn't have any hills. On this hill I come across a cat. So young its eyes aren't even open. It's lying by this pile of garbage in a puddle of water, somebody left him out there to die, just threw his ass away. I'm standing there looking at it, not knowing what to do. I don't need a cat, but I can't walk away. I guess I was supposed to rescue the thing. It looked sick, like you wouldn't want to touch it, but I did, picked it up. It was no bigger than my hand. Noises it was making was telling me it was about to die. I was gonna have to get something like an eyedropper to feed it. So I start walking down the hill to save it, but I wake up.

Then I just lie there feeling bad, wishing I could have dreamed the dream long enough to have done the job. Thinking I wish somebody would come and rescue my ass. And for some reason I start to laughing. I don't know what was so goddamned funny, but I couldn't stop. I fell back asleep and didn't dream anything, which is usually the case. When I woke up next time it was night, and time to go to work again.

Before I go, I eat pie. I buy blueberry or apple—I don't like seeds. Not every day, but about two times a week I do it, then sometimes I go a month without even thinking about it. My habit is to eat half of it and then the second half the next day. I like the first half best.

So I'm in the window eating the second half, watching what looks like a Negro lurking around down in the alley. I've seen it before, we all have. A man on crack or who-knows-what, maybe some crap he found in the back of a pharmacy, got dosed up on a bottle of pills that melted his brain pan. Anyway, he's moving around down there, looking through the garbage. Not till I get out my flashlight I use for fishing and shine it on him did I realize who it was. He didn't even look up. But there he was with my light on him, his big head, bare-footed still. Maybe he was looking for shoes. I had an old pair, tennis shoes for fishing, which I never did anymore. Where was there to fish, the East River? I threw 'em out the window, one after the other, didn't even look to see where they landed. Probably hit him in the head. That was time number three.

What happened at work that night clinched it. Big Al never comes downstairs, too important, got his own private mirror in his office. He could've combed his hair up there, but in he walks, steps up to the mirror, and starts combing his hair. I sit on my stool watching him, waiting, and without even letting me know he knows I'm there, he washes his comb, dries it off, puts it back in his pocket, and says, Lock the door, Spence. I lock the door. Then he takes out this paper sack, lays it on the counter, starts bringing lottery tickets out of his pockets, new ones, putting 'em in the sack. Must've been a hundred grand worth.

He tells me, Take the sack upstairs. There's some guy in a green suit sitting with a blonde at the end of the bar who I'm supposed to hand it to and without letting anybody see me do it. The whole thing was fishy. I'm hesitating, and he gets this smirk on his face, gives me a wink and says either that or suck his dick. No way is Big Al a faggot. He came down to put me on the spot. If anybody's ass was gonna get burned handing over that sack, it was gonna be mine. But I had no choice. So I took the sack upstairs and gave it to the guy in the green suit. But that was it, far as I was concerned; my probation was over.

I go back to my place. I make a call, find out about the bus schedules. I get my fishing pole from under the bed and put my stuff in a bag, then take the back stairs down to the alley. And guess who I run into—the Negro. I wouldn't be surprised if he'd been there since the night before. He's wearing my shoes too. I've got big feet for my size, and for the size he is, which is a lot taller than me, he's got small ones. The point is, is they fit him. He spots me watching him and I light out for the bus depot.

After about two blocks I look around and there he is, following me like a dog. I couldn't shake him. Followed me right into the station. I get up to the window to purchase my ticket, he's so close behind me I gotta whisper my destination so he doesn't hear where I'm going. Being pissed off at a guy like this is a waste of time. What was I supposed to do, holler at him, call a cop? I go around him wishing I hadn't of thrown those shoes out the window. I sit on a bench and wait for the announcement. He's five feet away, standing there looking like he's waiting to see what else I'm gonna give him.

When it comes time to board, he follows me out to the bus like he's gonna get on it. But to do that, you gotta have a ticket. He tries to get on, but the driver won't let him, pushes him back out the door. I take a seat to the rear so I can be alone. When I glance out the window, there he is, standing there looking up at me, got something in his hand, lifting it to show me. I put my nose against the glass to see.

What I see is he's got a fist full of money, a whole roll of it. Turned out they were hundred-dollar bills. You pay as you go in this life; if he wanted to go, who was I to stop him? He didn't seem to have any faith in himself, and that's where it all started. Him and me going down to Mississippi together. I got off the bus and got him a ticket with his own money.

First step in a good relationship is paying attention, making sure you're not missing something. In this case it was simple. What was there to miss? I put him next to the window and took the aisle seat for myself. He sits real stiff, very erect, eyes forward. But after we're on the road awhile, he starts making this little noise. At first I thought he was saying "pot," but after he said it a bunch, I figure what he's saying is "mot." So Mot it is, that's what I call him.

Because we had time to pass, I decided to try and interest Mot in a couple of topics. I tell him about the money I made telemarketing when I first came to New York. How the Jew who ran the outfit shortchanged me on my commissions, and how I called the attorney general on him. Next thing, he gets shut down, goes to court, goes to jail. Don't fuck with Spencer Hooler, was the message there. Next I related the story of how, when I was a kid, me and Doc killed my sister's cat. Put it to sleep on the dining room table and cut it open to see what it was made of. That was back when Doc had notions about me growing up to be a doctor. Then I tell him about being a barker in Doc's carnival. The next thing I know, the sun's coming up, and I notice my traveling companion must've done something in his pants. Some of the other passengers seem to be aware of it too. I'm about to take him to the toilet they got in the back, but the driver got wind of it, yelled for me to stay where I was, that he'd pull into the next convenience, I could take care of things there. And that's what we did.

It's barely morning, already hot. The hum of this big swamp cooler in the café makes it kind of homey. I take Mot to the men's. He seems depressed from his

HAMPTON FANCHER

accident. I try and tell him it could've been avoided, but he's not paying attention, must've been the bus that confused him. But with a little help, he pretty much knew how to do what it took to fix himself up, and we go back out. Being in the south now, I gotta say, our arrival did draw a little bit of attention. We sit at a booth, and I order coffee and toast. Had to butter the toast for him, almost had to feed it to him, but he got the idea.

The waitress treated us kind of snooty, then I hear her giggling with the cook. After that, she comes over with the bill. I tell her I'm gonna give her a tip, only one she's gonna get, which was, whoever's in charge of keeping the men's room clean was not doing the job; it stunk in there. She didn't like that. Either did the cook. He comes over, asks me if I got a problem. I tell him the men's could use some attention. He asks if I'd like to take a crack at it myself. I thank him for the offer, but tell him I got a schedule to keep. So he asks me if I'm an authority on the subject. I give him one better, tell him I'm an inspector for the Department of Health and Sanitation, making a tour of the area. He glances at Mot, says, I suppose your sidekick there gives you a hand in your labors, eh?

Nope, I picked this poor soul up at the last stop. Going back to the county lab to run some tests on him.

That stopped him, and I finished off by saying loud enough for his customers to hear that I hope he keeps his restroom a bit more tidy in the future, that I wasn't gonna write him up this time, but I'd be sending some-body back within the week to have a look. I give 'em a wave good-bye over my shoulder and guide Mot out the door.

W e crossed the state line into Mississippi that after-noon, and by then I realized old Mot was not gonna talk. Not because he didn't like me, but because he wasn't capable of the art. But things can get said without words, like with a dog or a mule. So by the time we got to Townsville, I felt like we kind of under-stood each other. Plus he definitely needed somebody to make sure he wasn't taken advantage of. People in trouble should like the ones who help 'em, but I didn't see much of that, not at first. But it didn't stop me from doing what I could. I took Mot home.

We lived out on Military Road. Reason they call it Military Road is because this same road was used by Colonel Merrick Starr when he brought in his troops to fight the Battle of Wood Creek, which he lost and which is now Wood Creek Golf Course. Back then our place was more a plantation, but over the years and because of the savings and loan people, it got smaller. By the time Daddy died and Mama married Doc, it was barely an acre. Some of it fenced, some of it magnolia trees and dogwood with a two-story house made of bricks mostly. We're about four miles from Townsville; it's what's called a poverty pocket. Only one taxi. We took it.

When we got to the house, Auto the mule was out front, saw us coming, and ran around back. Maybe he didn't recognize me. It had been better than two years, and he was about eighteen, so maybe his eyes or his memory was going bad. But for our arrival I pulled a good one. What I did was put Mot in the front door, rang the bell, and hid in the bushes. Took her a while to answer, but when she did, Sister is looking at this big black dude who doesn't state his business. Most women see a guy like him staring at 'em, they'd slam the door, call the cops. But Sister is tough. There I am in the bushes, trying not to laugh, and she steps out, goes around Mot.

I know you're out there, she says.

She prides herself on what she calls a sixth sense. I never go along with it, but I kind of halfway believe it too.

How'd you know it was me? I say.

Who's your buddy?

She means Mot, who got left standing in the doorway.

Just somebody I'm taking care of.

Not taking care of him very good.

That's because Mot just walked into the house.

He just wants some water, I say.

Fact is, I don't know what he wants. She goes in after him. He's in there watching the TV; one of those African animal shows was on. Sister asks him what the hell he thinks he's doing. She doesn't get an answer.

I distract her by asking if she's got any photos of Mama's funeral. I know she does, she takes pictures of everything. All I needed to do was hang on till sundown, which it almost was, and things would get better after she had her first highball. Then we could iron things out.

First, I wanted her to understand I didn't come back to take advantage of anybody. About how I got chewed up in New York City and would've been buried like a bone if I'd stayed up there. She tells me it's a cruel world, that's why we have traditions. That's why the firstborn, which is her, inherits the house, and I don't get shit. Said I'd had the chance to prove my life was worthwhile, and I failed.

After her second drink, she's telling me she's the one with the values in the family. Kind of singing her words now instead of saying 'em. I get the subject changed by asking how Doc is. Find out he's not running the carnival anymore due to his lung condition, got this asshole name of Jack LaHand doing things. Considering my professional intentions, that was bad news.

Then she's back on me again, accusing me of wanting to take advantage. I was about fed up with that, so I told her, why would I want what she has when I got what I have? And real snooty she says, Oh, and what could that be?

She walked right into it. I pull out the roll, give her a look at those hundreds, said it was my pocket money.

HAMPTON FANCHER

Boy, that shut her up. But just for a second. She wants to know how come I have it. Business deal, I said. Which is true, because Mot needed me to manage it for him. Then she starts singing a different tune. I mean opera that she does on the piano. Not just barnyard crowing either; Sister could have been a famous singer. This is always how she winds up the night, and after about highball number four she passes out on the couch.

Mot paid attention to the music while it lasted, but now he's back on the TV. The solution to that was to turn it off. I give him a bowl of soup and a Popsicle, then go up to my old room, put him on the floor next to my bed. I'm thinking about Mama's car. It's a Buick convertible, 1969 Electra, black with red leather upholstery. It's out in the garage—at least I hope it is.

Next I go to picturing Auto, thinking about his inner needs. I know he's got 'em. Thinking about the difference between us. That difference is what makes him worthwhile. Mot is worthwhile, too, for the same reason, because he's worthwhile to me. Thinking about this worthwhile business must've put me to sleep, because the next thing I know, it's morning. Mot's standing at the foot of the bed looking at me. I'm lying there looking at him, wondering if he's wondering about anything. Wondering about his breakfast probably, but he's not getting any. We gotta get out of there before Sister's up.

She's not downstairs on the couch, must've crawled up to her room to finish sleeping. The keys to the Buick I spotted the night before, hanging on a nail in the kitchen by the cellar door. But not now they're not. Well, I don't trust her either. I give Mot a piece of bread, go back upstairs, and sneak into her room.

I don't see the keys. Sister's lying there in her clothes all twisted and wrinkled. No way am I going through her pockets. On the nightstand next to the bed I see a little box. What I find in there is Mama's teeth. Sister might've hid the damn keys, but so did somebody else, and it's right then while I'm looking at the teeth I remember the magnetized hide-a-key Mama kept under her car just in case something like this ever happened.

The garage is really an old tobacco shed, big and dark with exposed beams. We're about to go in, but Mot stops, he can tell something besides the Buick is in there. What it is, is Auto standing in the shadows, looks like he's admiring the car, and it comes to me what the problem is. He's an unloved mule. Sister wasn't treating him right. He wouldn't even look at us, and that animal sparked a feeling in me. I give him the old mule whistle to get his attention. He still won't look at us, but his ears do some twitching. Then, real cautious, he comes over kind of sideways and slow, and then—bango!—quick as a snake he kicks Mot in the stomach, and would have again if Mot hadn't of been knocked to the ground, would have trampled him too if I hadn't put a stop to it and chased him outside. Auto goes running off across the yard, headed for the swimming pool. Mot's on the ground holding his stomach. I get him to his feet, put him in the car, and away we go.

I take the long way to avoid going through town, don't want anybody seeing me yet. Past Meg Picker's Trailer Court and hang a left on R-16, which leads to Doc's the back way. Sailing along, no traffic, the road narrow and nice, got one arm rested out the window, the other on the wheel. The air's already hot, it's getting mucky, but the sky is clear, makes me feel like singing.

"There's a bird that's small and nudgy . . . Perhaps you have heard of my favorite bird . . . the budgie?"

We pass a runaway car crumpled into a tree, been there since before I left. I wave at it like an old friend, but I can't even remember who was driving. For sure he was drunk. This is moonshine country. Not too many trees left, but lots of stumps. I see the old sawmill, slow down for a look, but it looks closed; the windows are all busted. We pass a field of muskmelons with a double-wide and an iron darky painted white beside the door. I glance at Mot. He seems to like driving down the road at a good clip; got his head in the wind, eyes almost shut and his mouth open.

Up ahead, some fellows on the side of the road, about three of 'em. I give a honk as we pass. For sure they know the car, maybe got a look at me, maybe didn't, but I bet they seen my passenger. They're KKK, picking up discarded trash to help the county, doing good works to improve their image.

Doc's place is a lot newer than Mama's. It's made of stucco and concrete, the windows are little and so are the rooms, and instead of grass he's got gravel. Says it's easier to clean. He's got dogs, had 'em when he lived with us too. Before him and Mama divorced, Auto killed one of 'em. Doc took a bullwhip, called it a mulewhip after that, and beat Auto pretty bad with it. The dog that Auto nailed was harassing him all the time. Doc says the dog was bred for it. Tobacco was a herd dog, thought his job was to boss other animals around. But Auto was a star, didn't like to get bossed around. He was a big attraction at the carnival, was a diver, used to go off a fifty-foot platform into a barrel of water. But after Doc whipped him, he stopped cooperating. Never did any diving after that, and didn't like dogs anymore either. But he still liked the water. That's why Mama had the pool put in.

Doc is hard to surprise. When we come through the gate, he's already in the doorway, his dogs slinking around, snarling, mainly at Mot. Doc wants me to leave him outside, doesn't like too many people in the house, it agitates the air. I notice he's got a new rig for his emphysema. The tubes go into his nose from his belt, where he's got the tank attached. I leave Mot outside, hoping the dogs won't care there's a strange Negro in the yard.

About the only decoration in the house is two pictures on the wall done by a quick-sketch artist who worked the carnival. One of Tobacco, the hound that

HAMPTON FANCHER

Auto killed, and a portrait of Doc himself. Both of 'em in charcoal, which I like. But right then I was overly concentrating on what to say. Before I can say anything, Doc screams, Shut up! The dogs are making a big commotion out front.

I ask how the carnival's doing. Shitty, he says. I'm starting to ask him about getting my old job back, but he cuts me short, tells me there's bad news and worse news. Bad news is that Jack, the son of Wolf LaHand, is running the carnival, that he's the manager now. Worse news is that, to save on money, the job of manager and barker has been combined.

If I was hearing it right, what he's telling me is Jack LaHand got my old job. That guy's no barker. Doc thinks maybe I'm talking about the dogs because he yells, Shut up! again. I tell him a deaf and dumb guy would be a better barker than Jack LaHand. He hasn't got the personality, no pepper in his hole, the guy can hardly talk, for Christ sakes. He uses a mic, Doc says. I just shake my head, then say, How come if he's not qualified, you gave him the job? Doc says he's sick of that question, but he's gonna answer it anyway. But first he wants me to go out front, make sure Mot isn't harassing the dogs.

I go out in the yard to see. The dogs are barking and growling, trying to intimidate Mot. But it's not working because Mot's giving it right back. He's taking the initiative, barking louder, growling harder than they are. If he hadn't been so big and loud, they'd tear his ass to pieces, but these dogs never ran into something like this. Your basic spade-headed hounds is what they were, about six of 'em, cowards, even in a gang. Mot really had 'em riled, the biggest of 'em snapping at the air, foaming around the mouth. Then Doc comes out to see, taking it in awhile before yelling at me to get Mot out of the yard and put him back in the Buick. Of course, now that his boss is here, the big dog's gonna show his courage and goes for Mot, but Doc whacks him in the head, grabs him by the throat, and that was that.

Somebody once said that luck was when the world says jump and you do. Even though neither of us knew it right then, me and Mot were about to be taking that jump. I put him in the Buick, then go back in the house to let Doc finish up his story. What it was is Doc had gone fishing with Jack's dad, Wolf LaHand. They spent most of the day not catching a thing, except according to Doc, Wolf had himself a lot to drink. Out there under the sun in an open boat on Lake Oakitobi, it's not uncommon for people drinking to go crazy. So on the way home Wolf decides he wants to ride on the hood of the car. But since that's how accidents happen, and Wolf was so insistent, Doc thought it best to lock him up in the trunk. Doc had a few himself, but he was driving fine, everything under control, and would've been perfect if they hadn't got rear-ended by a truck.

By the time the Jaws of Life had been brought in to get Wolf out, his legs were no good, and neither were his intestines. But still, I didn't see how come Doc had to give Jack the job. Must be something he's not telling me. To show I'm on board, I ask him to tell it again. He does, but this time it takes longer because every few words he's gotta interrupt himself for his breathing. But after it's over, I figure the point of it is that Doc felt he owed Wolf something, even if the accident wasn't his fault, because Wolf is in a wheelchair for life and wears a bag on his hip to catch his business. The upside is, there was a settlement from the truck that hit 'em, and Wolf bought himself a brand-new boat.

I guess Doc was ready to be alone now because he asks me if I'm going over to see Jack. I tell him I suspect I might. He stares at me a second, then he says, You still got some of your hair, Spencer. But if you're going over to see Jack, I'd get it cut if I was you. I thank him for the advice and take my leave.

Even though Mot was good at this barking like a dog, the trick of it was to get him to do it on command. My conviction is that anybody can learn anything, change what they are to what they want to be, and Mot was shaping up to be what I'd call the Wild Man. The question was, did he wanna be the Wild Man? The way he was acting back at Doc's, I figured he did. He had what it took; we'd just have to work on it. So while it was still fresh in his mind, we stopped in a field.

What seemed to work wasn't so much words as gestures. For instance, if I did the "dog" myself, he'd do it back. Then what I started doing is give him a little punch at the same time I'd want him to bark, and he put the two together. I detected something in his eyes then, something not so much dog as puppy dog, and I found that at that moment if I'd lift my hand to him, he'd cooperate. Actually, he was a quick learner. One session is all it took. At the end of it, Mot, I recall, seemed fairly pleased with himself. I know I felt pretty good about it.

The barbershop's a place where on Saturday everybody hangs around, even after they get their hair cut. Some boys don't even get one, they just come in to make fun of each other and tell stories. But it's not Saturday. Nobody there but Beck. I sit Mot in one of the chairs so he can watch. Beck throws a sheet around me, acting like he'd seen me the day before, like I never left town. He's a mouth-breather, smokes too much. I tell him he looks like a man who better lose some weight, get some exercise. He tells me he'll cut my ears off. That's the way we talk. Next he wants to know what kind of cut I want.

A New York cut?

He's trying to be funny, snipping at the air around my head with his scissors.

Just cut it, I tell him.

Beck himself is bald; must've figured being bald was bad for business, because he wears the sorriest excuse for a toupee you ever seen, must've sent in for it.

I ask him how it's going. He tells me that cutting hair for twenty years in this town is like printing counterfeit money in prison. I think he thought he said something funny, but I don't get it. I look at the wall; it's covered with pictures, a couple new ones, mainly sports and naked girls. Mot's got his eye on what's left of Beck's lunch. A doughnut and a half-eaten salami sandwich. Then Beck tells a joke. I don't laugh, tell him I already heard it. What about your friend, he says, meaning Mot. I change the subject, ask where Clovus is.

Clovus is a big black kid who was his sweep-up man. I find out he went away to college on a scholarship, which brings Beck to the topic of Mot, comments on his size. Says he's even bigger than Clovus was. I figure by Saturday Beck is gonna spread the word. Guess who's back in town? He'll say, Guess who he had with him? Old Spence, you say? Got a nigger who can't talk? They'll talk all afternoon about that one. Let 'em. Beck leans closer, got another joke.

You know why dogs don't like blacks?

I don't wanna know, but he gives it to me anyway.

Because they can't swim!

If you think that's funny, you're a bigger bozo than I thought, I tell him.

He thinks that's funny too. You can't win with Beck. But getting the haircut turned out to be part of a bigger plan. All the hair on the floor accumulated because Beck has this idea that the floor just needs sweeping once a week. Till it mounts up, why bother? Tells me he sweeps it up on Fridays. It's Thursday, so there's a lot of it. Mot's staring at it, giving me the idea. In a way you could call it Mot's idea, because it was him that gave it to me.

When he's finished cutting my hair, I ask Beck for a garbage bag and a broom. Beck's watching me sweep up the hair, trying to figure a way to charge me for it. Finally he says, What you gonna do with all that hair?

I tell him, Southern hair is worth big money up North. They got doctors up there who make wigs out of it and sell 'em to bald guys down South. He's so dumb, he doesn't know a real joke when he hears one.

Next I take Mot to the hardware store. We buy a big tube of roofing tar and take our project back home. So I don't get bothered by Sister, I turn off the engine and coast into the backyard. I get Mot and the stuff I acquired out of the car and into the barn. I need privacy, but it's so hot in there I leave the door open a crack. They say curiosity killed the cat, but Auto is a lot more curious than a normal cat. He's standing out there with his nose in the door, watching everything we do.

Once I get Mot down to his shoes and underwear, I start in with the tar. Keeping his face pretty much in the clear, except for his head, I give him a good coat of it. That stuff, if it gets on you, is hard to get off, so I use an old pair of gardening gloves to do it. After that's done, I go into my bag of hair, using handfuls of it to cover him with. It wasn't easy making it look like it wasn't something just picked off the floor and stuck on

HAMPTON FANCHER

to him. The way I did it looked like it was growing right out of him. Kind of bushy-like, like a bear that got himself plugged into a light socket. Turned out so good, in fact, I wanted to take him to a mirror, but didn't wanna stir up Sister by bringing him indoors, at least not till his tar was hard. Next I locate a blanket to put on the seat of the Buick so we can drive to our appointment.

Out in the daylight he looked even better. But he was acting kind of confused, so I had to locate a rope to tie around his neck to help guide him. Next problem was put the top up or leave it down. The sun is what I was thinking about. On the other hand, maybe the tar would protect him from it. Tar is black, and so was Mot, so I figure leave it down. And while I'm fixing that blanket up tight like a seat cover so there's no damage to the Buick, here she comes.

First of all, she wants to know what's going on. But a woman who spends all day wondering why she's alive and the rest of the night drinking I doubt could get a quick understanding of something like the Wild Man. In fact, she's so surprised by what I done with Mot, she doesn't say diddly about the car. She never drives it anyway, doesn't have a license for it because of her record. When she's finished hearing my plan, she goes off about the rope, doesn't like it around his neck, says it's dangerous. I need it to keep him from falling behind, I tell her; plus it looks good. But she has a point, so I take it off and tie it around his waist. It was my confidence that took the wind out of her. Her and

Auto just standing there watching me and Mot drive away to our meeting with Jack LaHand.

Out where the carnival is the land is flat, nothing out there except the carnival. Even from a distance you can see it, especially if it's night. You can see the rides lit up against the sky. That's why Doc named it Skyland. Skyland stays open all year long because the lake is pretty nearby, and the lake never closes. They got the hotel out there and other little places you can stay for people who don't have enough money to take a vacation someplace better. Fishing and speedboat rides you can do just so much of, then it's, let's go over to Skyland, go on the Tilt-A-Whirl, take in the sideshow. Also, the carnival's a good place to bring a date to.

In the afternoon, especially if it's not the weekend, there's not much action. But still there was some people hanging around and the lights were on, which was a good sign, except that they were flickering, which is how I knew Jack would be in the generator truck.

On my way over there I show Mot the Ferris wheel and point out one of the big cats asleep in his cage. Mot seems to have more interest in animals than in people. He was looking at that lion like he knew him, when up comes Funny the Fat Lady. Funny isn't fat enough to be the fat lady anymore. Besides, the real freaks stay out of sight because why pay to see 'em if you can see 'em for free? Cotton candy and apple-dipping

HAMPTON FANCHER

is what she was doing these days, plus running some rides.

She gives me a hug, then steps back, giving Mot the once-over, says, Whoaa! Whatcha got there, Spence? The Wild Man, I tell her. Tell her we're on our way over to see Jack, and she fills me in. Tells me the deal on the new acts, three of 'em. One's a contortionist who's a Bulgarian girl, an acrobat basically. Does her show on two chairs in a bikini and is a pretty good draw. Then this old guy by the name of Harold Peerson up from Florida, he plays dead. Lies in a hole, and the hummers—what we carnival people call the customers—watch him to see if they can catch him taking a breath. He looks deader every day, she says. But the big attraction is this guy from Brazil. Calls himself the Swallower. Puts a live white rat in his mouth, swallows it, then puts a big snake in there that goes down his throat and swallows the rat. That's a pretty good attraction, I say, a swallower that swallows a swallower.

There's lots of drunks in this line of work. Duke the Midget was a drunk and still is, far as I can see. I knew him as a clown, but before that he was a wrestler. Wore his hair in a Mohawk and did his wrestling to tom-tom music. But he was no Indian. In fact, he wasn't even a midget. He was a dwarf, but didn't like the two D's on his billing. I see him standing over there by the genera-tor truck with a pipe wrench, sneering at me. It goes back to a fight he picked with me before I left for New

York. One thing you don't wanna do is get down in the dirt and wrestle with a dwarf. Not only doesn't it look right, but the center of gravity is not in your favor. My thought was just punch him, get it over with, but he came in low, had me around the legs, trying to knock me down on the ground so he could put a hold on me. That's what forced me to kick him. Sounds unsportsmanlike, but he'd been kicked by bigger guys than me. He even jumped the Giant once, an eight-footer from Iceland that was also a drunk and stomped Duke in the head so hard he knocked out his eye. That's why Duke wears a patch over it and dresses like a pirate when he's not working the big top.

Word travels fast in the carnival. All I had to do was stand there waiting for Jack to come out, which after about two seconds he does. My hope is Doc already called him, but it turns out I gotta handle it myself. I start out sociable, ask Jack how his daddy's doing. He tells me Wolf is great, couldn't be better. Jack's being sarcastic. I inquire if Wolf still sells war souvenirs at the playground. Not every weekend anymore. What he does is oversee things now, Jack says. Bayonets, medals and badges, flags and uniforms, you name it, Wolf sells it, featuring mainly German regalia. He's telling me all this without so much as glancing at Mot.

I came by to show him the Wild Man, I tell him. So he looks at Mot like it's nothing special, tells me they already got a half-animal, half-human performer. He's talking about Chicken Man, and before I can tell him

Doc already sanctioned this deal, we're onto an argument about the damn Chicken Man. Who wants to see some fat white guy dressed up like a hen with a plastic beak? He says people are used to the Chicken Man, he's a familiar sight, tourists are comfortable with him. I say, Sure they are, he puts 'em to sleep.

Things are heating up because this is more than just about the Chicken Man, it's about what happened to his daddy, it's about Doc. And about me going off to New York. I tell him, Go call Doc, straighten things out, but Jack doesn't like being told what to do. He's standing there working his jaw like he's setting up to do something he'll be sorry for if he tries it. I see Duke the Midget smiling at me, hoping it's gonna hit the fan so he can jump in with his monkey wrench. Fine, let him. Then I whisper, You wanna tangle with the Wild Man? Say the word, Jack, all I gotta do is . . .

I give Mot's rope a little jiggle, leaving it to Jack's imagination about what could happen next. It's getting serious now.

You making me a threat, Spence?

I lean forward smiling at him, I say, You get between a dog and his bone, you know what happens?

Then what he does is whip out his gun, points it mostly at Mot. Mot doesn't give a damn, probably didn't know what it was. Then Jack starts backing away, going to the phone was my guess, but had to do it on his own terms.

I felt pretty sure that what just happened, happened

in my favor, so I guide Mot to the parking lot. And sure enough, not two hours after we get back home, Doc calls. He was drunk maybe, but from what I get out of it, we had a conversation that said Spence Hooler and his Wild Man were in business.

I felt good about how things went, so when Sister comes into the kitchen with her bottle, I had a drink, gave one to Mot too. He swallowed it straight down; then about six seconds later, without any warning, he throws up. Something he ate that the gin must of triggered. Falls to me to clean it up, and when I finish I see Sis is making a study of him. I was glad to see her take an interest. Of course, that's always how it starts, a family gathered around itself before it turns into trouble.

I tell her how I'm gonna have to locate a man-size cage to put him in for the show, put a blanket over it to hide him from the hummers to build up the suspense. She objects to the whole idea, says nobody wants to be covered in tar and put in a cage with a blanket over it. Says she thinks Mot is depressed, wants to take him somewhere for an "evaluation." I tell her I gotta go upstairs. Tomorrow was gonna be a big day.

Up in my room I stand Mot next to me, and facing the mirror, I start practicing ideas. The first thing about being a good barker is knowing psychology. Get their attention, make 'em wonder if maybe you got something nobody ever seen.

"There are things in this world nobody can explain. Observe and marvel, ladies and gentlemen! Under this blanket I have a creature that medical science would like to get its hands on. He eats raw meat, live chickens! And if I can't get him any of that, he'll chew the grass, eat the worms right out of the dirt!"

Then I'll whip off the blanket, and the question then is gonna be, will Mot perform? Will he have the heart for it? And right then, like he was inspired by our little rehearsal, he starts gnashing his teeth, growling like a dog, wagging his big head around. And I knew we were in business. Best to save our energy for the performance. I call it a night.

Next day was lots to do. First thing was make sure Mot wasn't left to go wandering into Sister's attention, because I had no time for complications. And he couldn't be left in the yard either, because I'd caught Auto nibbling at his tar. So I had to lock him in the barn for the day while I attended to my appearance.

I went down in the basement, go through what's left of Daddy's belongings. First thing I find is a little box. I think what's going to be in there is cufflinks, but what's in it is a rattle off a rattlesnake Daddy killed. Daddy's clothes are stored in a cardboard box. Suits, shirts, and shoes. I try on a checkered coat. It's thick and got leather at the elbows, but it's the right look, and a tweed cap to go with it. There's gloves too, soft Italian ones for driving with. And a cane covered in snakeskin I'm going to use to point out the importance of what I'll be saying.

I go up to find Sister to invite her to the show, but she says she hates the carnival, even if her own brother was gonna be one of the main attractions. She makes a comment about my outfit, doesn't like that I'm wearing Daddy's clothes. I feel like saying, Hey, you wanna wear 'em? Go ahead. But there's no point in it.

Okay, here's what happened. We get to Skyland on the early side so I can get certain details settled. For instance, I gotta arrange for the cage, so we go on over to the office first. That's when Jack tells me some crap about being over the limit on platform space. Says it's state regulation, and if an inspector comes by, that's it, they've had it.

Who says? I wanna know.

Doc, he tells me.

I say, Bullshit!

He says, Call him.

I do. Called him on Jack's bastard cell phone. When I heard it from Doc I started yelling, telling him I wanted paperwork on this, something in writing. Telling him, You don't go around dropping somebody out of his job without having a legitimate reason for it. He says that I never had the job in the first place. I remind him it was all sewed up the night before on our phone conversation, but Doc can't remember it. Drop Chicken Man, I tell him. Me and the Wild Man will take his place. But it turns out Chicken Man has a contract. I tell him I'm getting a lawyer on it, and he hangs up on me.

I can hardly believe it, but I do. That's the kind of crap that happens down here. I even bought a big chocolate cake so after our opening me, Mot, and Sister could celebrate.

When we get back home, I join Sister in helping her finish off her nightly bottle. Seeing the cake was a sad thing. Me and Sis sat there drinking the gin, not talking much, just watching Mot. Watched him stick his finger into the icing, testing the taste, then watched him eat the whole damn thing. I knew what was gonna happen, so did she, and we were right. He threw up. This time we cleaned it up together.

I was fired up on all kinds of dirty tricks I wanted to play on Jack. I didn't blame Doc so much as the La-Hands. I knew they had him over a barrel. And when Sis heard enough about my ideas of getting even with those needleheads, she went off to bed. But I couldn't stop, and there's Mot sitting there, staring at me like he knew what I was thinking. I'd taken my thinking about as far as it would go by sunup. Then I knew what I had to do, and it had nothing to do with setting fire to Skyland. What I really needed to do was what I'd been dreaming about doing for a long time before all this ever happened. So I take myself a shower, wake up Mot, and drive us out to the lake to go fishing.

But an excursion that starts out simple can pull you right out of what you expect into a fate you never dreamed of.

TEETH

The shoppers and the merchants were gone. The silence of leftover noise, of leftover smells, was strong. Everything closed. Almost dark. It was Sunday.

The horse's head above the horse-meat shop. The machine that made it cannot be imagined by the man looking at it. But nothing is a waste, he thinks, for him who will touch the bottom of no matter into what he falls, and he thought of the Arab girl. Saw himself as a restless tired bird, her as an island.

Later in his cool sheets waiting for the noise of morning, he imagines her sitting alone somewhere eating, and vaguely all the other functions of her body, running sure as the cycles of the moon, like a rock or a cat. The little hairs of her body stood out like stars in the dark of his love, and he made a note of it.

A page full. And after hesitating to throw it away, he threw it away, then bit into the skin of his wrist so hard the impression of his teeth remained for a day.

If he knew her, there would be nothing he couldn't tell her, nothing he wouldn't show. He was sure she was noble. He liked her hands. Here all alone from Algiers, he liked to think. Proud. Expecting nothing.

Actually she was from Jerez de la Frontera. She was Spanish. She'd been in Paris almost a year. Worked at the confectioner's washing dishes and silverware up the narrow steps on the second floor where they had a small counter and tables.

From her window above the street she watched him standing in front of the horse butcher's, looking up at the plastic horse head. Her stomach was empty. Her fingers went to the scar on her abdomen. She rubbed her belly through the cotton shirt. Two years before she had awakened with a pain like fire and it didn't go away. At work that morning, finally she could no longer walk, and was taken in a cab to the hospital and operated on.

They found teeth in her belly. She didn't want to see them. The doctor said they were little vestigial teeth. She tried not to show her fear so he wouldn't tease her. He would have if he thought she was better-looking, and told her that it was not unheard of to find such things, probably left over from what might have been her twin. It sounded nasty, and when she went to her village the following Christmas she was afraid to tell her mother, but she did. Her mother said nothing.

There was still light in the sky, but the streetlights were on. The street completely empty. The man had gone. She didn't like to go to bed so early, but there was nothing else to do. At least this way she would sleep through her hunger, wake up and go to work where she could eat. She drank a glass of water from the bottle and lay down.

CONCORDE

t rained. To get out of it he went into an English-language bookstore on the rue de Rivoli. Glancing through some Stephen King, he noticed a sign and a stairway that led to a smoke-filled tearoom with uncomfortable chairs and poor service. He took a table next to a young American girl eating bread and a salad. A redhead—not the orange flaming kind, but darker and cut short. She was tall, had a slim strong body with the hands of a boy and a redhead's firm, almost opaque skin.

Her face was sharp, sensuous, alert, easily given to irritation. Or ecstasy, he thought. A touch of consternation on the forehead. Nothing blurred; she was exact, she was radar. She was reading a French magazine, but he knew she wasn't French. It was her shoes. They were scuffed, well used. This girl was an American who had done some walking.

"You ever had a fire in your refrigerator?"

That was a good line. Stupid, but unique. She'd have a mind that might appreciate something like that. She would respond:

"You mean stove?"

"Depends on what you keep in it."

"Like what?" she would ask.

"Artwork."

That would be good. She might ask him if he was an artist. No, she wouldn't—she wasn't an asker. What was she? Student? No, Ph.D. maybe. Maybe just on vacation. Maybe married. Nope, no ring. Boyfriend then. So what?

He could ask her if she knew Tartini.

"Tartini who?" Or maybe she would know. No, she wouldn't know. He'd have to tell her. Italian. First half of the eighteenth century. Composer, violinist. "The Devil's Trill." Fuck Tartini, she'd think he was a nerd.

He watched her eat. She used her teeth like she didn't want to get her lips in the way. Gave her a kind of snarling affect. This girl was against her own best gift, constitutionally. What gift?

To give, to be true, to be known. She lacked goodness. She had it, but didn't have a clue how to live with it. She confuses it with compromise. A lady, sure, but still a teenager. Her own way or no way. A sensualist, but her trust was pinched. Her hunger, her sentiments, be damned. Yet he could see that there were mountains of it. A woman with sympathies she can't express. Her sweetness rotting in the brig. She loved so strongly she couldn't live with it, is what he decided. But so what, not acting on your best qualities is like not having them. But he needed something from her. Needed her to look at him, to want to know him, to help him. He needed her goodwill.

Humor was the way: "A lot of people die on the toilet. A friend of mine's wife just did." That he had a friend who had a wife might help. It was a lie. But it was a grabber. "Lenny Bruce too, he died on the toilet." That was true. Then maybe in a barnyard voice he would say, "I tol' you not to go in the outhouse, Billy, Grandpa's busy. / No he ain't, Ma, he's dead!"

How would she respond to that? She's too young to remember Lenny Bruce. Maybe she read a book about him. He could tell her he knew Lenny's mother. That was true. And then she would go back to her salad. She ate fast, like she grew up with a brother who stole her food.

He pulled out his pen, started writing on his napkin. *enraged depressed touch of self-hatred boredom too. dread of her own feelings. helplessness. tenderness. masking it.* He turned the napkin over: *accentuates her insolence with makeup to ward off the weakeners. a woman of resolve . . .*

He looked up. She is looking at him, she looks away.

She made him think of a cricket pitcher pacing off the distance and throwing the ball all the way to hell. She looked about twenty-five. He is fifty. He keeps writing. *suppressed unmet wants unappreciated . . .* He paused. Where was her curiosity, her creativity? Taken away, replaced by learning?

His coffee came, but no cream. There was some on her table.

"Could you pass me that cream, please?"

"It isn't cream."

"What is it?"

"You don't get cream in Paris. It's canned milk."

That was bullshit, but he wasn't going to argue with her. She went back to her magazine.

He stared at the wall, at the other people. He felt warm. He thinks about putting money down and getting out of there. She wasn't somebody he'd like to sit around a fire with. He glances at the cream. Then at her. She's not looking. He takes a quick sniff. Maybe it is canned milk. He reflects on the way she passed it. She did it with distance, but she feels close.

He knows she is fearless. But she will never drop the mask. Maybe in bed. If so, this, this is why she feels close. But she is terrified of being embarrassed. She will take no chances, not of the heart. She needs music, painting, poetry. The great abandon. She is faithless, but faithful. This is why he knows he could love her. She doesn't believe in a thing. Except not to submit.

He could tell her about the dog in his building who waits by the elevator for someone who is going to the right floor. It's a hit-or-miss proposition for the dog. Some tenants know what floor he lives on. But sometimes he gets left on the wrong floor. The dog can't open the door to the stairway either. His owner is senile. There are so many things he would like to tell her.

He waited for her to look so he could say something real. Or maybe it would be her who would speak. Tell him she has a weakness for men who have secret jobs. "Like spies?" No, she isn't talking about the CIA. Tells him she saw a fat guy once who worked in a bookstore, the kind of place professors and writers and fervent women went. That the fat guy looked like a dirty dumb giant, like he'd be better off on a farm, but it would turn out he was a poet. He would have sent her some of his work. How did he get your address? She wouldn't remember. So what's so secret about him? But this was not a girl you could press. He'd better say something real. What was real? The unreal. He could tell her about that.

"You ever felt like you might lose control?" That could scare her, but it would make her look up and listen. "I have fantasies about hitting strangers in the mouth. I get these feelings like one time I'm going to get one of these terrible, totally inappropriate urges that are not really urges, they're just these awful feelings that mean I wouldn't be what I am if I followed through, if I actually did it." "Did what?" "The unthinkable, and I get a kind of sweat inside myself like dizziness and suddenly I'm terrified. Not because I'm angry or frustrated, but just because all of a sudden what if I became something I couldn't stop, something I didn't want to be, something I couldn't explain to myself?"

For the first time she would smile and say, "Like the wolfman?" And they would laugh. "No, not like the wolfman. More like the panic an epileptic might feel just before it happened." And she would nod. She would understand and he would be in love for as long as he lived. The insecurity was so intense, but they would have understood each other. He would reach under the table and she would close her fingers around his hand. She would know he was an idealist and could not accept anything as it was, and she would hate that because he would never let her be.

Out the window he saw the rain had stopped. She was paying her bill—took care of it in perfect French. He put money on the table and followed her down, through the door and into the street.

He walked behind her and thought about her crying. But he couldn't really see it. "I cry a lot," she would say, and he would believe it. She went into the Métro at Concorde, and as they were going down the steps, she ran ahead and he hurried to get to the bottom before she beat him.

THE FLAME
AND THE
ARROW

He never got away with anything. If he stole something, he was caught. If he lied, he was found out. If he sneaked into the girl's room, he was reported. But that year there were two things he did get away with. The second one was major. The first one was just gum.

He had climbed up on the kitchen counter with no other purpose than for some routine snooping. He found it on the top shelf between a stack of dishes and a bag of something he didn't bother to open that felt like salt. The gum wasn't just a pack of five pieces, it was a jumbo pack with smaller packs inside it. He'd never seen anything like this. Dentyne, bright red, sealed, untouched. He could smell the minty cinnamon of it even unopened. Somebody had hidden it for themselves, hidden it from him.

Duke was at work, his sister not home yet. Only the maid was in the house. She wasn't really a maid, but that's what he called her because it made her mad. She was his mother's aunt Anna and came on afternoons when nobody was home. He wasn't trusted in the house by himself. Bud was seven.

By nature Anna was sympathetic, it was hard for her to be strict. When he crossed her, consternation was the best she could come up with. Bud was tricky, he bewildered her; truth was, she found him irresistible. And he knew it.

He climbed down from the counter and went into his parents' bedroom. Anna kept her eye on what she was doing, but knew he was in there. He went into the closet, and yelled, *What's that?* The Hoover is too loud. Look! Anna turns off the machine. She can only see his back in the closet.

What's that? he whispers. Wary, she comes closer. Bud is pointing down at the pile of shoes in the back. He tries to grab her to hurry things along, but she doesn't want to be hurried. He steps out, giving her room to go in. Down there . . . see? Anna steps in.

She's not much taller than him, but twice as wide, also old, complains of sore feet and arthritis. Squinting, she stoops for a closer look. Bud shoves her as hard as he can. Anna goes down.

He slams the door, locks it. Trapped, she begins to pound and scream, demanding to be let out. I'll tell your father! And in Spanish too she yells it, then her muffled voice pleading, Please, Buddy! But Buddy is already in the kitchen, crawled up on the cupboard, tearing open the gum, stuffing the little wrappers into his pockets, the pink tangy tabs into his mouth. He's balanced on the edge of the counter, chewing like a squirrel, hears her voice becoming more desperate.

She might go nuts if he doesn't let her out. The family due home any second. The ball of gum getting too big to chew, and he's got another pack to go, but no time. He scrambles down.

I'm gonna let you out, Anna!

No doubt she heard his voice, but not the gum-garbled words. Bud runs out the back door. The ball of gum, still leaking sweetness, but he spits it into his hand and, hard as he can, flings it over the back fence. Puts the unopened pack in his back pocket, then changes his mind and throws that too.

A change of climate, the advent of a season, subtle as they were, made Bud want to migrate, and it frustrated him that he couldn't. Behind the house was an alley that went almost a mile, and at least once a week he would go all the way to the end.

The next day, he's out there, not for a trek, but to retrieve the unopened pack. He can't find it, not even the ball of gum he already chewed. A dog? A bum? He hoped it wasn't another kid.

Feeling gypped and uneasy, he waits to be indicted for what he's done. But it must have been forgotten, or blamed on someone else, he doesn't know, and never will. Anna's ordeal was so terrible she didn't speak of it, or she's not a fink. Bud decides on the latter and stops calling her the maid, for a while.

At school he is an outsider. At home he feels at home, but still an outsider. Where he is not an outsider is when he is alone. The Flame and the Arrow is a club of one.

He painted the name in red over the door. In the alley he scavenges items of interest to decorate the unpainted walls. A stringless ukulele, a rusted tin lid of a candy box embossed with a faded Queen Victoria. A barrel he had found, rolled in, that once in a while he uses as a toilet. The place had a fetid smell, made it less inviting to guests. Bud didn't want guests.

Rawn wasn't allowed in the Flame and the Arrow. She had her own playhouse, and he wasn't allowed in hers. It was a whitewashed plywood room with little windows, a chair, and a dresser with a mirror she liked to sit at and look at herself. She called this place the White House. Nobody else did. Nobody called it anything. But they referred to Bud's playhouse as the shed. A shed is all it was.

Nobody was sure at that point, but it would turn out that this was the last year of the war. McMurray was too old for it, but said he was in a war two wars back. The Spanish-American. That's how he got his limp, was wounded in the battle of San Bledo, is what he told Bud. Told him not to tell anybody. Bud didn't. Just Duke and Rawn. She didn't care, and had nothing to say. But Duke did, said the old man was lying.

McMurray smoked Old Golds, always had one in the corner of his mouth. The paper at the lip end soaked with saliva, his nose, which was narrow and fine, always ran. His eyes watered too. He wore gray khaki pants and shirts every day of the week, newly washed and always ironed. Bud figured the old man's sister,

Miss McMurray, did the job. Mostly she kept to herself, had headaches, had to stay in the dark a lot, is what Bud heard.

There was gossip too. The McMurrays weren't really brother and sister. Bud believed they were because they looked alike. And why would they say they were if they weren't? Rawn didn't know. He asked her if she thought the two of them, when they grew up, would live together. She ridiculed the idea, but he could tell she liked it too.

McMurray's limp was from the hip down and the knee didn't bend, turned his walk into something like a swagger. Once Bud told McMurray he recognized him from a block away, because of his limp. Proud of himself, he told his parents. Instead of approval, he was admonished for it. They wanted him to go over and apologize. Go next door and tell old McMurray he was sorry? Even he knew that wasn't going to work for anybody. Still, his mother said it was not something to brag about. Brag. He had bragged. He wasn't positive he knew what it meant, but had an idea and didn't need to hear any more about it. Then Rawn had to tell him something too. Said what he'd done was "crummy." He tried to punch her. She punched him back, then went into the bathroom and locked the door.

McMurray told Bud he had been a first sergeant in the 8th Cavalry, stationed at Fort Bayard, New Mexico, served with Black Jack Pershing in the one against the Mexicans. Bud told Duke. Duke said McMurray was lying again. Why? Because he was afraid of what was waiting for him. Bud wanted to know what that was. Duke said it was rubber underwear, a wheelchair, and if he's lucky, a nurse. Duke said that if he were McMurray he would kill himself. Bud wanted to tell McMurray what his father had said. But he didn't.

McMurray was the air raid warden. A self-appointed position, as it turned out, but Bud didn't care, the old man had the hat. It said AIR RAID WARDEN in black letters across the back. He had a long flashlight too, and when there was an air raid and the whistle went off, McMurray hobbled up and down the street, shining his light in people's windows, making sure they stayed in the dark. Bud had seen him do it.

McMurray had no use for a car, long ago turned his garage into a workshop. Like Bud's shed, it was made of unfinished wood, but his had a little window and was organized, tools hung neatly on the wall, from large to small. Above the workbench there was an array of cubbyholes containing his collection of rocks. He would pull down the shade, turn on his special lamp, show Bud how some of his rocks could glow.

Once McMurray told him that Miss McMurray believed that two twelve-foot lizards were in control of the universe. Bud was pretty sure that's what he said. Sometimes it was hard to tell; McMurray had something wrong with his throat, had to clear it a lot; his voice didn't always catch. Bud didn't know what to say, but it was an image that would stick in his mind. Who knew what lizards that big were capable of?

How come Duke wasn't in the war is the only question McMurray ever asked Bud, and he answered it himself.

The reason your dad ain't in the war is because of his eye. Bud never thought about it till then. Never thought of Duke as a one-eyed man. Never thought of him not being in the war either. When he asked, Duke said he tried to join, but was past the age limit. Also that they like to leave some doctors at home so people can get taken care of. Did he wanna go in the war? Yeah, he did. The eye didn't help, is all he said about that.

Duke drank gin out of a shot glass. Bud had one too. Gin looked like water and that's what Bud got in his glass. When Duke was in the mood, they would have a drink together, clink their glasses. To the war!

And there were pictures, photographs of pictures really, little ones, that McMurray showed him. Naked Indians on horses at night circling cowboys, shooting at them with arrows. The Old West. McMurray had been there too, had fought the Apaches. Bud wanted one of those pictures. McMurray said he would give him one later (he never did) and went on to explain the difference between unconditional surrender and an armistice. Bud liked unconditional surrender best. So did McMurray.

Sometimes Bud was tempted to let McMurray in on

his Nazi activities, but had the feeling he should be careful. Air raid warden McMurray was long and thin, had a hunchy back, but strong. Bud could feel it when they shook hands. Sometimes the old man would grip him by the neck to help him see an ingredient in one of his rocks. The oldest one he obtained was from a punitive expedition in Mexico. Punitive expedition. Bud liked the term. It meant going somewhere to punish somebody, McMurray said, and in that case it was a Mexican killer by the name of Pancho Villa.

Generally Rawn kept her distance, but once in a while McMurray would catch her, invite her into his workshop. She was too polite not to go, but she didn't like it. Never were she and Bud invited together. The neighbors on the other side, the Georges, never invited them to anything. They mostly kept to themselves. Mr. George managed the local gas station, was a patient of Duke's, and Duke took the Buick there. Mrs. George had bright red hair and wore shorts with pockets in them. Mr. George called her Babe.

Bud had never had a chance to talk to her. She waved at him once. He wanted to marry her and planned on doing it when he was older. The Georges had no children, but they owned a Chihuahua named Taco. They burned his droppings in their incinerator. Bud's mother used to shut the windows on trash-burning days and complained, said she was going to take up a petition. The smell intrigued Bud, but he didn't care for the dog.

Most of the houses on the block had something beside lawns, incinerators, and single-car garages. The Georges also had a tortoise called Roy. Bud wanted it, but it had a chain through its shell attached to a bolt in the ground. The yard had a small fountain that Mr. George had built, and on the grass around it there were six of the seven dwarfs, made of concrete. But no Snow White. Happy was also missing. Bud liked Grumpy best and tried to steal him once, but Taco made such a fuss he couldn't get away with it.

A good thing to do in the night was climb up on the roof of the Flame and the Arrow and watch the Georges through their windows. Sometimes he could see them in bed, looking at the radio. One time he got Rawn to climb up with him, but she didn't like watching and he never asked her again.

In those days a large percent of the killers and loonies were overseas fighting the war, and parents were not so nervous about their kids being outdoors at night. At least Duke wasn't.

Sometimes Bud would be missing from his bed by morning. Rawn would find him curled under a coat on the floor of the Flame and the Arrow. It should have got him in trouble, but Bud was always liked. Duke once told him he couldn't be whipped. Bud thought he meant spanked. No, Duke said, it means you can't be beat, it means you can't lose. Bud didn't believe that. There wasn't a day went by he didn't feel like he was losing. There was something that wasn't there and he knew it, knew it was somewhere else, but he couldn't get there. Duke said, You might be a liar, but you got integrity. What's integrity? It's what you got inside you that never says uncle.

Duke's brother, who everybody was proud of, was a major in the Army. On what is called a furlough, Dick came to visit. Brought his two children from the city where they lived so he could drink with his brother and tell war stories. Bud and Rawn would stay up and listen, but his little cousins didn't get to. The son was four and puny, his sister, high-strung, bit her hand when she was upset. Bud wanted to hurt both of them. Take them up the alley and kill them. They only stayed a week.

Twyman, the boy, had a tic. Duke told Bud the medical term was echolalia. Under his breath, after anyone said something to him, Twyman would repeat the last sentence. Bud was intrigued and tried it himself for a while.

That was one good thing; the other was that Dick brought them all presents from the war. A German air raid curtain for Rawn. She was supposed to have a coat made of it. For Duke, a big bottle of English gin. And for Bud, a German bayonet and gas mask. When Dick left, he forgot his combat boots. Bud snatched them immediately, hid them in the Flame and the Arrow. They were too big for walking in, but he did it anyway. He would belt the bayonet to his waist, put on the gas mask, and, still wearing his shoes, slip his feet into the combat boots.

A little secret of himself is that a part of him wanted to be killed. President Roosevelt and the government would catch him, tie him to a chair, take turns slapping him. But he wouldn't talk. They would have to shoot him.

Twice that year after everyone was asleep he went on secret missions. Once, out into the street, to an all-night diner, wearing the gas mask, so no one would recognize him. There were two customers at the counter. They took an interest. Bud dropped hints about his mission. The cook gave him a free doughnut, advised him to watch out for MPs and the Shore Patrol, and shook his hand when he left.

Sometimes Bud would go into his mother's stuff. Duke hadn't changed anything since she went away. There was a drawer with a bunch of silky things he liked to look at and put to his nose. But he was disdainful of Rawn's underthings. The big bras and how they made her act. Her body bothered everybody, her most of all.

At twelve she was flat-chested, but as she bloomed, she developed a bad disposition. Stuck-up is what Bud called it. He wasn't sure if it was an act or not. She knew it was, but it wouldn't let go of her. Rawn was depressed. Depressed enough to kill herself, but decided to hold on to see if she would be a movie star first. She spent lots of time thinking about being famous, but everything that made it feasible she resented.

She wanted people to look at what she had, but hated it when they did. And when they didn't. Bud was comfortable in his own skin, and she envied him for it.

They watched each other without the other knowing.

He watched her primp and she watched him conjure. Bud had the power to make people feel good or make them feel bad. He didn't mean to, it just happened. And mostly with Rawn. They didn't get along, but no one understood them better than they understood each other. Bud could say that stick looks like a gun and she would see it in a second. But Bud couldn't be trusted. If he could use it, whatever it was, especially a secret, he would. Rawn knew she couldn't trust him, but she wanted him to love her too much not to tell him. He wanted to know what McMurray showed her when she went into his workshop.

She said every time it was the same. He would pull down the shade, get out the box. What box? The box he wants me to smell. He would take off the lid and put it under her nose. Rawn would hold her breath and pretend to. What was in it? demanded Bud. Shit, Rawn said. You see it? No! she said. You don't have to.

McMurray was weirder than he thought. Funnier too. Rawn acted disgusted, but it made both of them laugh. That night, in their bedroom, Bud needed to hear it again. He wanted more, wanted to know why McMurray did it. Rawn didn't care why, she didn't like being questioned and told him so, told him to go to sleep.

But he pressed it. She told him to shut up. Bud told her that her tits were too big. She almost hit him, but came up with something better. The reason their mother left was because she couldn't stand being the mom of a smelly little savage like him and she was never coming back.

One thing Rawn wasn't was a snitch. Bud was. Not an outright tattletale; he was slyer than that. But nobody ever believed him. Everybody believed Rawn. He would get even by making her feel worthless, bring her low self-esteem lower. *She was the smeller of the box.* His plan was to expose not only her, but throw McMurray in as well. And that's what he would have done, if the war with the Germans hadn't of ended.

Before Duke told him the news, he saw it out front, in the street. The traffic stopped, drivers honking, some out of their cars, yelling and hugging each other.

Bud wanted to know if all the Nazis were killed. Duke said they were pretty much done for. Told Bud not to worry, before he grew up there would be a new war. In the meantime he could be a cowboy and kill Indians. Bud didn't wanna be a cowboy. The other war, the one with the Japanese, was still on. It was even closer. All he would need is a good rowboat. Bud knew he was being made fun of, but it was okay. He knew Duke, in his funny Duke way, was trying to make him feel better. Then be an Indian and kill cowboys, he said. Bud didn't want to talk anymore.

The next day, things got better. Three blocks up the street was Theo's Sports Shop. Bud liked going there; smell the guns, look at the knives, the bamboo fishing poles. But what he never looked at before was the hunting bow. Lemonwood, Theo said. The first costly thing Bud had ever needed, and he knew it was out of the question. No way he could ever ask for that much money. Either he would have to steal it or steal the money to buy it. Or just wait and will it to come to him. But he can't. He wants it now.

That night, after everyone is asleep, he sneaks into Duke's wallet. There's enough money in it for the bow and arrows. But to steal from Duke was the act of a scoundrel. So he just took a dollar and went back to bed.

When he wakes up, before he knows anything, before he even remembers the bow, he remembers something he forgot he knew. The money Rawn has been saving from every Christmas and birthday she ever had is hidden under the paper that covers the bottom drawer of her dresser in the White House.

It was a real hunting weapon, and there were two steel-tipped arrows with black fletchings that went with it. Unstrung, the bow was almost as tall as Bud. Twenty-six dollars. Bud had twenty-nine and change. Theo folded his arms. He had never sold anything like this to a kid. It was like a gun, except you didn't need a permit.

What are you gonna do with this?

Give it to my uncle when he gets back from the war. He's a colonel.

A colonel?

The one just before a colonel.

A major.

Yeah. He wants to go to the mountains and hunt like the Indians, is what he said. My grandmother gave me this. He pushes the money forward . . . So I could get it for him.

There was something wrong, but Theo wasn't sure what it was. Then he decided there wasn't.

Bud wanted to run, but knew it would look suspicious, so he walked fast. By the time he got to the alley, he was goose-stepping. Then he ran. Went into his yard through the back gate.

He didn't know where anybody was. Who was in or out of the house. He held his breath, listened. All he can hear is the occasional passing of cars out front. Ruthless is what he would be. An archer. Except he can't string the bow; the wood is stronger than he is. He tries to bend it, but he needs help. Not McMurray, he didn't want him in on this, and his sister was out of the question. So was Duke. Mr. George could do it. Bud stashes his two arrows and, fast as he can, walks to the gas station.

A bright warm day, Bud is in a sweat by the time he gets there. There's traffic on the street, but no cars at the pumps and nobody in the little office. He hears an engine running in the garage. Bud smells exhaust and the oily coolness of the cement floor as he peers through the entrance. But it's dim, takes a moment for his eyes to adjust.

He's never seen Mr. George on a motorcycle. He's sitting on it with the engine running, reading a newspaper. Bud comes closer, isn't sure how to proceed. He holds the bow out, its loose string dangling. Mr. George looks up. Bud standing there holding out the bow to him. Mr. George lays the newspaper across the gas tank, kills the engine, and without dismounting, takes it. This is a good bow you got. He holds it up, assessing the thing, and with an approving nod hands it back. Bud doesn't take it.

Could you make it work?

You want me to string it?

Bud's face is a mask, but his eyes are gleaming.

He watches Mr. George wedge the bottom end of the bow against his foot so he can bend it at the top, pull it down, and notch the string.

What you gonna do with this?

Put it on my wall.

Bud gets a pat on the shoulder and Mr. George watches him leave. Feeling better than he did before he strung the bow, Mr. George takes his paper and goes outside.

To test one of the arrows Bud sticks the point of it into the fence separating his yard from the Georges'. It's so sharp it easily penetrates the wood, and Bud is mighty pleased. Robin Hood accurate is what he wants to be, but lacks a target. He peeks over the fence. Lucky for Taco he is not in the yard. He spots Roy, but shooting a turtle is stupid. Might as well shoot one of the dwarfs. He considers it. He's not sure what he should do, but knows he better do it now. To shoot an arrow as high as he can into the sky is what he decides.

Bud touches the tip of his tongue to the fletchings for luck, then notches the arrow. Feet planted, knees slightly bent, his right hand draws the string back far as he can. He lets it fly. It goes ten feet, flounces on the lawn. Disgusted, he grabs it off the grass. Slots it again, with a tighter grip, draws it back, aiming above the roof of the house. Lets it go. The arrow sails over.

Thrilled, he slots his final arrow and, with more confidence, rocks back, face to the sky. Punches his bow hand out as far as he can, pulls back the string to his shoulder, and lets go. The snap of it bites his fingers; he flinches and grins, bent over squeezing his hand between his thighs, looking up, unsure if it cleared the roof, but he's not going around front to find out. He is done.

Bud tries to break the bow across his knee and is hurt a second time. Leverage is what he needs. A tool, something that will snap it in two to make it easier to get rid of.

One of the garage doors is slightly open. He's looking at the crack of space where the door is hinged to the wall.

He inserts half the bow into the opening, then grips the protruding part with both hands and pushes forward until it snaps.

Bud takes a spade from the garage and goes up the alley to dig a hole. The ground is hard, it's not easy. He thinks about saving the string, but buries that too.

Next to a garbage can he tucks the leftover money, three dollars and forty-two cents, into a pile of sand spiked with cat turds.

Rid of the incriminating evidence, but not free of the crime, Bud waits for the hammer to fall. But it doesn't; nobody says a thing. To cover himself, he considers telling Rawn he saw a tramp snooping over the back fence looking at her playhouse. He gives thought to becoming a better kid. Maybe one night he'll help her with the dishes. But never in his life will he regret getting rid of the bow and the money he buried. But never will he take an interest in archery either. The day after it happened he searches around in front of the house and scans the street. There were no arrows anywhere. It made him nervous to think what they might have stuck in.

He didn't hear any horns honking when the bomb was dropped on Japan. He heard it on the radio first and decides to have a look, take a walk up the street to see if anything has changed. Miss McMurray is out in front of her house watering. Her lawn is well kept, unlike theirs—Duke didn't care about the grass. She was tall and skinny like Mr. McMurray, but didn't smoke or smile.

She is vacant-looking, but vigilant; her body makes him think of a grasshopper. If he came too close, she might hop up and flutter away. He has never once talked to her, but for a while now he's been wanting to ask her about those giant lizards.

She stiffens as he comes closer. Certainly she knows he's there, but won't look at him. He feels embarrassed, closed out, and after a moment starts to walk away. Before he's taken three steps, he stops. She just asked a question. He turns to look at her. She's standing there with the hose piddling water, mouth open, her teeth small and yellow, her little eyes averted. He says, Pardon? She repeats the question. Her voice soft and harsh, like her brother's. Will he be a doctor like his father when he grows up?

This is a question other adults have asked. First he will be a football player, then join the Navy, and after that he'll be a doctor, is what he usually says. But now, he can't think of what to say. He's never seen her talk to anyone before. Except once. To his mother. It was soon after they moved in. From the porch he saw the two of them in the yard; Miss McMurray was watering again. His mother standing away from the grass, on the sidewalk, in white high heels and a black and white dress. And his mother threw back her head and laughed. He wants to know what it was that made his mother laugh.

But instead, he hears himself ask about the giant lizards and how it is they control the world. The universe, she corrects. Did my brother tell you that? Bud says that he did. Now she is looking at him and Bud feels the soggy wet grass penetrating his shoes. Almost in a whisper, Miss McMurray says that two twelve-foot lizards controlling the universe was not her idea, and turns away.

RAT HALL
JACK

The house sits on an uneven acre, eighty yards from the road, forty from the creek, and twenty from the tree. Rat Hall was built a hundred years ago. Jack has seen a hand-painted photo of the place dated 1891. The giant sycamore in front, exactly the same. There is an owl that lives in that tree. Crows and red-tailed hawks in the day. A lizard or two on the patio usually. Coyotes, squirrels, and occasional snakes to be seen. All this a half hour from a freeway that can take you wherever you might want to be in the city of Los Angeles. Jack never locks the door.

Rat Hall is in ruin. One day it will either be torn down or made over, but Jack likes it as it is. The living room is full of windows, but not much light. Knotted vines of wisteria obscure the glass. There are holes in the floor, in the ceiling, and spots on the walls where lathing shows through. The scent of Rat Hall is cool like mortar, a blend of wood and the dank fragrance of the old fireplace, occasionally the sweet whiff of desiccated rat down from the attic. He bought the house two years ago with the patrimony from his father's death. A suicide.

In the bedroom there is a crack in the linoleum. With a flashlight, Jack can see the dirt of the earth below. He likes to feel like the house, himself, and the ground beneath are all of a piece. But still, he doesn't like thinking about what might come out of that crack while he sleeps. He's had a bunk built five feet above the floor to put his mattress on.

There had been a second house up the slope behind Rat Hall. It burned down fifty years ago. Its foundation and a small pile of rotted lumber are all that remain. Jack calls this place the Platform. In spring and summer, naked but for sandals, he climbs the broken stairs to lounge in the sun, do push-ups, a bit of yoga maybe, sometimes with pen and paper, in case he gets an idea.

Except for what the wind does to the leaves of the trees or the scream of a hawk, the distant hum of a car on the road below, Rat Hall is a quiet place. A good place to write. This is what Jack is trying to do, trying to write a book about his father. But for over a year now, no matter how hard he struggles to sort it out, coherency eludes him. But the solitude of this little world suits him, being alone with his music, his books, watching the lizards, free to do what he does within the parameters of his capacities. Also, Jack has a woman. She is thin and tall, long-eyed, with a neck like Nefertiti. Stewart is severely beautiful, quietly kind, a simple girl really, with an even disposition, and except for an occasional glass of beer, doesn't drink, has never taken drugs. Her Chinese mother was an Anglophile who insisted on using her husband's middle name for her daughter's first. Stewart Pritchard makes money on her looks—she is a model.

On the cover of *Vogue* is where Jack first sees her. A week later, in person. A friend invites him to a gathering that turns into a bash. Stewart arrives in the thick of it, attracts attention. Jack keeps his distance, but through the shifting din of heads and shoulders, their eyes meet. It lasts five seconds. Stewart is first to turn away. Next time she looks, he's gone. This is something he is good at. But before he leaves, Jack gets her number from the host. The following day she is surprised and glad to hear from him.

And the day after that they go to dinner. He brings her back to Rat Hall. Not something he usually does with strangers. But they don't feel like strangers. Sitting next to him on the balding velvet cushions of his couch, she looks around. Except for a little blue landscape tacked on the wall, the living room feels like a place for a tramp or a ghost, something abandoned. It frightens her a bit, but not the man. Stewart is intrigued with Jack, feels he understands her, feels herself at home in his eyes.

He asks if he can see more of her, all of her. It takes her a moment to understand what he means. She stands, watches him watch her take off all her clothes.

Sit down over there, he says. Wonderfully nervous, she sits on a single straight chair. Quietly, almost reverently, he asks her to spread her legs.

You are the dream, he tells her, half Venus, half housewife. It is true. She radiates loyalty. Jack goes to her on his knees. He lips her lips above and below. Inside her, he whispers she is the loveliest place he will ever be. So simple how he says these things. That he could live in her beauty forever and that he can't and that he will, at least he will try. Never has Stewart been as happy with a man. Jack tells her she is the one since childhood that has beckoned him.

Stewart buys a sprawling ranch house up the road. She loves the canyon, but Jack knows she wouldn't have done it if he didn't live there. After a year, he realizes she is not as simple as he thought. She is on antidepressants. He never asks about the bite marks on her hands. He doesn't want to know. He knows enough. She wants to keep something to herself, but it is hard. She has to tell him everything. A mistake. Jack doesn't like the likely, the probable; only the impossible could be perfect.

Stewart senses his disappointment and tries to please him, and the more she does, the more disappointed he becomes. He begins to see evidence of something he thinks of as small-heartedness. A lack of wit. She used to laugh at the tricks he played with words, but she no longer inspires him. Her last job, or the story of her day, has ceased to interest him. They make love accordingly.

HAMPTON FANCHER

He has become a ruffian in bed. The authority of his sex is as much as she can get, so she takes it and participates voluptuously.

Only once did she become outwardly angry with him. At a birthday party for her agent, Jack told the man's wife she shouldn't have fixed her nose, that a large one was better than a ruined one. Afterwards Stewart accused him of arrogance and insensitivity. Jack argued his case, had to have the last word, and ended it with a laugh. She never got angry with him again—not the kind that spilled itself. Jack tried once in a while to provoke her, so he could give her the benefit of the doubt, redeem himself, but she never again gave him the chance.

One night over dinner he suggests they should see other people. He isn't thinking of himself, he says, but she knows what it means. It means he is tired of her. There is a photographer who has been calling, who doesn't stop asking her to dinner. Peter Ryles, a South African, famous for shooting retired dictators, thirty-foot crocs, and the world's most beautiful women. He is in Beverly Hills for a week doing movie stars. Jack encourages her to accept the invitation, tells her he needs time alone to reflect on his father. The book, she says. That's it. Jack is once more a free man, unburdened from the duties of love.

He keeps a hatchet sunk in a stump next to the fireplace that sometimes he takes up to the Platform to throw at a tree. He's never gotten it to stick, but it's exhilarating to try. He is up there hurtling it when he sees the snake. It's at least five feet long and black as licorice.

Exposed, but easy in its own display, the old rattler is making its way across the Platform. Jack comes closer. The snake hesitates an instant, then continues. Jack baby-steps alongside it to the edge of the Platform. The snake slides off the concrete into the dry yellow grass and disappears under a stone beneath the pile of rotting lumber.

He could have cut its head off with his hatchet. The snake could have coiled and bit him in the ankle. Instead it has slithered into a hole, but not completely. It has left about a foot of its tail exposed. Jack counts the rattles. Eight. He waits for it to disappear; it doesn't happen. With an index finger, Jack touches it. The silk of its ebony skin, like the smooth coolness of a gem. But alive.

Suddenly, without a thought, he pulls the snake back out into the light. It whips around, lifting its head to strike, but Jack has stepped back out of range, rubbing his hand as if he'd been bitten. Coiled, but not rattling, the snake waits to see what will happen. Jack thinks about the rats in his attic and wishes he could give it one. He is inspired. You are one hell of a decent snake, Blacky. A snake of distinction. Blacky slowly uncoils, slides back to his hole. Jack knows something important has happened. The oak rattles. Jack looks up at the flickering leaves. He almost weeps.

HAMPTON FANCHER

On the floor, under the space of his elevated bed, he keeps a pomander of cloves Stewart had made and given him to keep snakes away, an old Chinese custom. But after his run-in with Blacky, he tosses it in the creek. It's more than simple fondness; he feels like Blacky is a harbinger of good things to come, the thrill of a riddle come to visit him. Blacky had been courteous for a reason.

Even though they haven't talked in three days, Stewart is still his closest friend, the one he needs most to tell his story to. He leaves a message for her to call him back. By nightfall she still hasn't. By midnight he stops leaving messages, at four a.m. he stops calling.

She once said she would do anything for him, loved him so much she would even have sex with another man if he asked her to. But did she love him so much that she *wouldn't*? The night is hard passing. At nine a.m. he brings the phone to bed but is afraid to use it. He will wait until noon. Just before twelve it rings. He hears the difference in her voice. Jack tries for nonchalance. Did she just get home? Stewart never lies. Did she spend the night with Peter Ryles? She did. That was fast. Yes, it surprised her too. Did she have an orgasm? Three. There is nothing to be done. She is sorry. Jack wants to see her. She has to get some sleep. Dinner? She's promised to have dinner with Peter. He is only in town a few more days. She is sorry. Jack needs so much more than that, he needs to see her. Stewart needs to sleep; she has a fitting at the end of the day. She hears an imploded sob. She waits. Jack? He throws the phone against the wall. It breaks. He tries to find the old phone. A little voice at the bottom of him says, As soon as you get her back—if you can—as soon as you do, you know you won't want her. But that voice doesn't stand a chance. He finds the old phone under some shoes and calls her back.

In the next three days she will visit him twice. He will go to her place twice. But she won't make love to him. He will beg her to tell him she is in love with Peter and no longer in love with him. If she will just say it, he promises to leave her alone. But she won't say it. She says she's confused.

Feeling okay, doing well, things running smoothly, could never keep Jack's attention, but this trauma has legs. Howling at the moon resonates in the myth of himself. Stewart is decent, patient, and guilty, but knows better than to say yes when he asks her to marry him. She thinks it best they don't see each other for a while. He wants specifics. She wants time. Tomorrow is time. He calls her. She says something about too little too late, but gets it wrong. He is angered on both counts, but mostly it's the cliché that pisses him off. He has the sense to keep quiet, bide his time, endure another day.

Jack comes up for air. First time in a week he stands naked on the Platform. Stomach in, chest forward, spine straight. The Tāḍāsana position. He contemplates the word. Pictures the line over each of the *a*'s, the dot under the *d*. Maybe he is wrong and this is the pose known as Vṛkṣāsana. Meaning erect like a mountain. He isn't sure. At least he's trying. He thinks about making juice, maybe going down to the beach. Right then, on the road below, he sees her car flash by, returning from another night with Peter Ryles.

Jack has had it. No place to turn except to her, and she is gone. He lifts his arms to the sky and sputters, Please let me die! Then collapses on the hot concrete and says it again. He hears the hum of the bees and doesn't care. The rasp of the oak leaves in the breeze and doesn't care. He wants death, so badly wants it he thinks maybe it has already happened.

He can't hear the bees anymore. The world has closed. But he hears something. Light as a finger running its tip along a length of silk, and it's coming closer. Jack turns his head, opens his eyes. It's a foot away, coming at his face. In a flash Jack is on his feet. His sudden rising causing the snake to coil. It's Blacky! He begged for death, death came, about to crawl under the hollow of his neck. If he hadn't heard it, he would have been struck. He stands staring down at the dark embodiment of his wish. Without so much as a rattle, Blacky unspools and slides past the man to the place he was headed, the little hole in the shade under the rotting lumber. This is where Blacky lives, thinks Jack. I was lying at the serpent's door.

Jack the fatalist believes life to be random. Turn right, you get hit by a bus. Turn left, you get laid. He called for death, death came. But he was saved. The ocean is twelve miles distant. Jack is almost two thousand feet above sea level, but suddenly he can smell its tang. Blacky has been a benediction. Jack can have what he wants, or not have it; either way, he is himself again. Stewart can hear the difference in his voice, adores the story about him and the snake. A week later they are making love again. She will marry him.

Jack has just taken her to the airport. A job in Trieste. She will be gone a week. He is relieved. He will have to address this marriage thing when she returns. He doesn't want to believe it couldn't be anybody, but knows it can't be her. For one thing she wants children. The idea of harvesting an infant in Rat Hall makes him laugh. He walks into the cool dim of the front room and abruptly stops. Blacky is stretched out on the floor in front of his bedroom door.

Thrilled, the welcoming host goes into the kitchen, pours a splash of milk into a saucer, brings it back, places it on the floor three inches from Blacky's incredible head. The thin black tongue slips in and out, reading the offering. But Blacky doesn't move; neither does Jack. It occurs to him that Blacky has come to stay.

Have you heard? Jack has a new pet. Stewart will tell all her pretty friends that her fiancé has a pet snake. Not a fashionable python, but a mean, highly venomous, five-foot rattler is what he's got, and he feeds it by hand.

Now Jack wants to lie on his bed, contemplate the

wonder of what has happened. He knows true faith will not suffer doubt. If he is to step over Blacky, it must be done in absolute compliance with the conviction that Blacky will not strike. Slowly, Jack slips off his clothes, inhales and exhales a lungful of *prāṇa* to integrate his *kuṇḍalinī*. He pictures the painting by Edward Hicks, of man and woman, lion and lamb, and all the green world in passive accord, *The Peaceable Kingdom*. Then, with his eyes closed, he steps over the snake and into his bedroom.

Jack rolls up onto his bunk, lies back to reflect. Spring and summer, Rat Hall's climate is favorable to reptiles. Rats from the attic scampering the premises at night—Blacky could get a plump one anytime he wants. And in the winter, the dark beneath the bed is perfect for hibernation. Rat Hall has everything a big snake needs.

In a reverie of connection to the nature of things, Jack recognizes that Blacky is no mere pet, but an actual avatar who deserves a proper name. *Blacky* . . . *Black magic* . . . *Merlin* . . . *King Arthur* . . . and there it is. He whispers, Arthur! and falls asleep.

Three minutes later, Jack opens his eyes, looks over the edge of the bed and through the doorway. Arthur is gone. He jumps down, steps into the dining room in time to see the snake sliding into the broom closet. No time for deliberation. Jack catches Arthur just before he disappears and pulls him out by the tail.

This time, the snake is in no mood for it, coils so fast

Jack hardly has time to jump back before it strikes. Stunned, Jack backs away into the bedroom. Arthur slithers after him. Jack jumps up onto his elevated bed. Arthur is coiled and buzzing on the floor, hammerhead stretched high and cocked. Come on! shouts Jack. It's me, calm down!

But Arthur's head is almost two feet off the floor now, weaving like a thing in heat, the terrible little gun holes of his eyes fastened on Jack crouching on the mattress. There is no way Arthur can get up to him, but Jack, infected with panic, looks around for something to bash him with. He considers the phone. Probably it would break. He would be phoneless again. Then he spots the horn hanging just above him on the wall. A German hunting horn, a legacy from his father. He lifts it off the nail. But this precious coiled horn is not for throwing. Kneeled on his berth, Jack puts it to his lips, aims it down at Arthur, and blows. The blast fills the room.

The serpent, of course, is earless, reads the oscillations with its tongue. Arthur is stunned; the shrill abruption in the air afflicts him, and fearing for his life, he hurries back into the dining room and slips through the barely opened door into the broom closet.

Horn in hand, Jack slides off the bed, peers into the dining room, watchfully crosses it. Slowly he opens the broom closet door. Just a broom and dustpan, a can of paint, and the rat hole Arthur squeezed through to a safer world.

Jack knows the consequence of love is loss. Loss is the figment that stalks the land, the sea, and the night; blood and hope, sex and sky, loss is the big bang itself. Jack returns to his bedroom, climbs up on the bunk, and hangs his horn back on its nail.

THE BLACK
WEASEL, II

On our way to the lake I meant to stop at Jack Master's bait shop to obtain some night crawlers when the right rear tire blew out. The spare in the trunk turned out to be flat, which was good with me; I didn't feel like changing a tire. Fishing was gonna have to wait.

It would have been about a five-mile walk either way, but it was too hot for that, so best thing was hang around till a Good Samaritan came along. That was not out of the question in this neck of the woods, and sure enough, in about twenty minutes, here comes Plaz Camel. I hadn't seen him or given him a thought in probably five years, and there he was, showed up exactly when I needed such a person.

What I was doing with a Negro covered in tar didn't seem to concern him. Probably he'd already heard something on that score, so we decided to go to his house because he said the gas station was closed but he had something in the automotive department I might like to have a look at.

I'd never been to Plaz's house before; it was a place like something a little old lady might own, except there was a '54 Chevy pickup parked in the front room. He tried not to show his pride in it, but it was clear that's how come he brought us over. I ask him how he got it inside. Took it apart out front, he said, hauled the chassis in sideways, then put it all back together. Took him three years, just an idea he got so went ahead and did it, he says. You could go in the Guinness Book of World Records, I tell him. He said he didn't like publicity, didn't wanna be famous. I understood that.

There was no room to sit anywhere except in the truck, which was the idea, I guess. Even though Mot's tar was dry, we had to wait for Plaz to bring out a couple towels to protect the seats before he let us get in. I never saw Mot stubborn before, but he wanted behind the wheel, and when I tried to push him over he wouldn't budge, so I let him have it. I sat in the middle, and it was kind of cozy all of us being in the cab together, Mot bobbing his big head, making motor noises, steering like he was going somewhere. I could smell there was gas in the tank and looked to make sure there was no keys in the ignition. Put me in mind of a story Doc used to tell about how it was he got circumcised back when he was twelve.

Usually it was not much more than a creek, but because of some storm the Kanakoli was all swelled up, Doc and his dad having a drive to town alongside it. Sometimes a younger brother was included in the story, so there was three of 'em. To impress his daddy, little Doc tells him how he's such a strong swimmer he could dive in the river and beat 'em to where it was they were going. Doc's dad, who was a tough old bastard, plus also a doctor, stopped the car and told little Doc never to say he could do something unless he meant to do it.

Doc told me he didn't really want to, but there was no choice at that point, so he takes his shirt off and dives in. Split his head open on a submerged log and would have drowned if big Doc hadn't of gone in for the rescue. Little Doc woke up in the hospital, and since his daddy was a doctor and since little Doc was in for one thing, why not do the rest like sometimes they did in those days? Stitched up his head, circumcised him, and took out his appendix. Three birds with one stone, and nothing he could do for quite a while that didn't hurt him, he said.

It could be that's how come Doc became a doctor, never again wanting any doctors to have power over making decisions about what happened to his body again. Every time he told that story he'd get tears in his eyes for being proud about how his daddy saved him. But not about the next part, which I didn't get to tell because right then something went wrong with Mot.

Started with a sneeze—not a little one, it made us jump. Next he's coughing, then he's choking, having what could be called a spasm, black stuff coming out his nose, him gagging and trying to get his breath like he was drowning. When something like this happens, you wanna get out of the way and hope it's gonna stop. But it didn't stop. Plaz yelled, Get him out of the truck! We did, but it wasn't easy. Plaz got clipped in the head by Mot's elbow, nearly knocked him down, and wouldn't touch him after that so it was up to me getting him outside across the yard and into the backseat of the car. All Plaz did was hold the door open. I used one of the towels stuck to Mot's back to wipe away what was coming out of his mouth, then it was step on it Plaz and we took off.

On the ride there I realized if Mot didn't get better it was gonna be partly my fault because of how like a child he was in his dependence on me and how deep my responsibility to his situation went. If he didn't improve, I didn't think I'd be looking forward to any birthday parties because life wouldn't be worth getting any older in. Dark thoughts, but down deep I believed Doc was gonna be able to fix him, because even in his current condition Mot was strong enough and good enough to beat this thing. On the other hand, if I was wrong, this thing might just go ahead and kill him.

Soon's we got into Doc's, I could see Plaz wanted to hang around, see what was gonna happen next, but Doc didn't like too many cooks in the kitchen. Neither did I. Besides, him being a stranger was driving the dogs nuts, so I told him to go home. I'd catch him up on what happened later.

Of course Doc could see he was in trouble, but before he could pinpoint the problem Mot had to be toned down. I held him steady while a shot was prepared. Doc gave it to him in the neck. That pretty much improved his condition, made him almost back to normal, far as I could see. But Doc said Mot was still in trouble, his skin couldn't "breathe." Problem was, if he peeled off the tar, Mot would be skinned alive and die like a snake.

Doc said the solution to this was what he called the solar petroleum treatment. Sounded fancy, but the principle was simple, about the same as getting an oil stain off the driveway, he said.

In the garage there was a five-gallon can of gas for emergencies, and that's what this was. By way of a ladder we got Mot up on the roof of the house. Closer to the sun, I suppose; didn't ask. Doc was a drunk, but he knew his business. We took off Mot's shoes and poured the gas on him. I used a rag to blindfold him, make sure his eyes were safe, and whatever was in that shot kept him calm as a kitten. Like Doc said, either the gas and the sun was gonna do the trick or he was gonna die. I went down and brought him up a bottle of cola in case he got thirsty, then had a good look around, made sure there was nothing that could cause a fire. After that it was a question of time and pray he had enough sense to stay put and not walk off the edge of the roof.

Doc didn't have any patients, so all we had to do was wait it out, watch TV, drink some beers. He wanted to talk about Mot, couldn't remember how I got him, so I told that story again, left out the money part, but not the part about saving him. Doc thought he bore a resemblance to Cassius Clay. Surprised I didn't think of it myself, because it was true.

Least I didn't have to worry about his safety, because the dogs were out there keeping an eye on things, knew there was something on the roof. If Mot started flexing around, they'd set up a ruckus. Dogs are nature's warning signals.

Doc used to have parakeets too. But they died. Instead of throwing out the cage or giving it to somebody with real birds, he bought two plastic ones. Not that he was sentimental; I think it was that he didn't want the cage to go to waste. The real ones didn't have names, but he called these plastic guys Cocker and Cohen. If you have something not real, he said, names help.

When I was a kid I had a teddy bear with a name. I used to have sex with him. And when I did, afterwards I'd tell him I was sorry. I was nervous somebody might catch on, so I cut a hole in his neck because I'd seen a guy with a tracheotomy, and told Doc and Mom I was practicing to be a doctor and that way they might not jump to conclusions about the hole I made between Roy's legs. Of course when I'd have sex I'd have to pretend Roy was a female instead of a bear. So in that case the name didn't help.

At sundown we went back up on the roof. Mot was on his back just like we left him. First I thought he was dead, but he was just sleeping. Didn't wake up too easy, but seemed glad to see me when he did. The sun and the gas had done the trick. The tar was all flaky and falling off, but some was still stuck on him in certain places. A water hose and a horse brush would do the rest. Because of Auto I had that kind of equipment, then some Ajax if it was needed.

Pleased with how it went, Doc asked if I wanted another beer. Two 'nothers, I say. Mot deserved one too. Then it's a question of how to get back home. Buick and the flat could wait, so I had Doc drive us, but he didn't come in. Me neither; took Mot around back for the cleanup.

Not wanting to call attention, I didn't turn on the floodlight; brushed him down and hosed him off in the dark. Got him close to how he was before the tar. It felt good to accomplish, but didn't make me feel like going in to answer questions about the Buick, so we stayed outside awhile waiting for Sister to go to bed. I sprayed Auto as well; he loves the water. Of course the water made noise, so probably Sister had a look through the window; maybe not, but if she did, she decided not to interfere.

Mot was done in from the hardships of the day, fell asleep next to the pool with Auto watching over him. That's how mules are: Once they show you who's boss, they'll treat you like family. So, figuring everything was too tired to make any trouble, I went upstairs and hit the hay. Tomorrow is another day, as they say.

Next morning I look out the window, see it's a bright gusty day, leaves blowing off the trees, and there's Auto standing by the pool, staring at something moving in the grass. It's a newspaper, wind flipping the pages over, making it look like he's reading the thing. He eats a page before the rest of it blows away. Then Mot comes out of the tobacco shed with a board stuck to his foot. Starts walking around in a circle trying to shake it off, and I go down there to see what's up.

One simple thing like a nail can change everything. Went right into his foot. Think of Jesus. You think he didn't howl, or at least cringe, when he got a nail pounded into his foot? Not Mot. When I pulled it out he didn't even wince. Hardly any blood either. Not to say he wasn't glad to be free of the board, but the thing was, he didn't feel any pain. To make sure of it, I gave him a pretty hard pinch on the arm. I was right. Mot somehow had gone beyond hurt. I bet it happened because of the tar, or the solar petroleum treatment, or the shot Doc gave him. Or all of those things—who knows? But I was starting to see an opportunity here. Not the Wild Man anymore, that didn't work, but this was a condition that had possibilities to it. A man who couldn't be hurt was a whole new story.

I could see the fans lining up to see it. Ladies and gentlemen, for five bucks you can kick him, hit him, work him over with a switch, jab him, or smack him. People handing up their ten-dollar bills to have a go at him. Scratch him, burn him, baseball players could slug him with bats, football players kick him, tackle him. For twenty bucks, ladies and gentlemen, see wrestlers throw him across the room, attack him with dogs. It could even be a TV show, call it *Give It to Me Now!* Some famous flogger in a turban and loincloth does push-ups, then flexes for the crowd. Let the flogging begin! The flogger's stick hisses through the air and Mot gets the beating of his life, doesn't even blink. Or forget that idea, he could do commercials. Tylenol, for instance. Who knows where this could lead?

Nowhere, of course. I wouldn't do it. A guy who felt no pain could really get hurt. But things cross your mind when you're developing an idea. It was gonna take some thought. Thinking about his side of it too. How's he supposed to learn about life if he can't feel any pain?

I decide to take him inside, make some waffles. Probably he'd never had one before. He deserved something special. I didn't say anything about his new ability, but after looking him over, Sister said she was glad I'd come to my senses and took the tar off him. I didn't tell her how it was done and she didn't ask, but it was true, he looked pretty good. Mot was an impressive specimen, natural-born muscles, scars and tattoos, fat too, but not the Jell-O kind—he was firm as an inner tube. After putting a bandage on his foot we got him into a jumpsuit that Sister got at the surplus store, a blue one, extra-large, but it was still tight on him—reminded me of the kind they wear in jail, no sleeves, which was nice because Mot had muscle-builder arms.

I couldn't find the waffle iron and she didn't help, acted like she didn't care, but I knew once I made some she'd eat 'em. Lot of junk under the sink is where I found it; also came across the bucket and snorkel Mama used to use to improve her looks. Nobody ever talked about it but we all knew it happened. She used to stand on her head in ice water to reduce the bags under her eyes. Something I guess she learned in a magazine at the beauty parlor, but it never worked. Once you got bags under the eyes, unless you do surgery, they don't go away. Upside down in ice water could've been what gave her the heart attack. I didn't bring it up; a subject like that might turn into a fight, so I went ahead and made the waffles. Put pecans in the batter. We had 'em out on the porch.

Sometimes something you think gone wrong turns out to be a good way to go; then just when you're about to get started, it changes again. What started with a nail ended with a bee.

I heard it, then I saw it; it landed on his arm. For being a slow guy, Mot had a fast hand. Swatted the sucker. There it was, dead on the floor. But it got him, could tell by how he looked, the way he rubbed his arm. To make sure of it I gave him another pinch right where he was stung. You could see it hurt him. Mot had his senses back. He was like the rest of us again. Mot was no longer the man who felt no pain.

Sister wanted to know how come I pinched him. Told

her it was an old Negro trick to cure insect bites, learned it from Doc when I was a kid. Not true.

Then she wanted to go back in, call the auto club, get the Buick taken care of, all whipped up and ready to go. Sister could do that: lay around for days, sit with her head on her knees, then—bang!—she's up and cleaning the house twice in a row.

What she does next is tell me she sent Mot's suit out to be cleaned. A thoughtful thing to do—fine, I agree, it'll be good to see him all dressed up again. The label inside the coat is what she wanted to discuss, says it was from some fancy deal in London. I knew that, and so what? I got stuff says *Made in China*, but that doesn't mean I'm Chinese. She's saying Mot is a man of money. Maybe, maybe not. Who knows where he got all that dough, the coat, his pants. Of course he had no interest in this, sat himself on a stool in front of the TV waiting for somebody to turn it on.

Then she's on the subject of his tattoos. I agree, they're not regular tattoos, not skulls and hula dancers. But she's making the case that they're "tribal," her point being that Mot was no local Negro. Of course he wasn't, I got him in New York. I could see where she was headed, but didn't give her the satisfaction—you let her win on one thing, next thing she'll have you washing the dishes.

She wants to take him down to Mister Fig, find out what went wrong with him. That's where we differ;

I don't care what went wrong with him. Everybody in the world's got something wrong with 'em, and finding out how come hasn't made any difference yet. Mot had less wrong with him than most people I ever met.

Fig was a so-called mind reader, who wore a necklace. Don't know why they call him "mister" unless it's because he's missing something. I said he was a shyster and no way was I taking Mot down there. She said "shyster" was a nasty word. I suggested she consider having a consultation with Mister Fig herself. But disagreements like this could cause her to lose control, so I tell her on second thought Fig might be a good idea, I'd think it over. But I wouldn't. This idiot worked out of a trailer on planks, covered in nut grass, probably infested with spiders and rats. I wouldn't go near the place, but I'd seen it. His specialty was olfactory perception. He'd sniff a customer up and down, then tell you how your ancestors were doing and, for more money, what the future was gonna be. All by how you smelled.

I didn't buy an inch of it, and it disappointed me she did. Sister always had an interest in black magic and self-improvement. I found a note once she wrote telling somebody she hadn't done the Rites yet because after she started in on something called the Klister Diet she was on the toilet too much to begin the program. She got kicked out of the house when she was eighteen for growing marijuana in her closet. Under the impression she had a job dancing in a nightclub, I hitchhiked all the way to Shreveport to join her. What it was was a strip joint, and she was a cocktail waitress. After she got off work that night we went up to her room on the second floor of a two-story hotel she got to stay in.

She was drunk and tried to read the Bible to me. Then this cabdriver showed up and I was told to get out for a while. He was a big guy with long blond hair, wore a yellow taxi cap. I waited in the hall, sat on the floor until they'd finished what they did in there. Then this cabdriver came out making noises through his nose like a goose. He tried to teach me to do it. Told me if I could get it down, my future would improve. He said it was a thing he got from a book about India, and if he wanted to he could be the president someday, and in a past life he was burned at the stake, and that the planet Earth was just a stepping-stone to a place with better-looking women. He was drunk and pretty pleased with himself. Gave me two bucks and a handful of quarters because I told him it was my birthday.

After he left I went back into the room. This was July—I remember because it truly was my birthday. I turned fifteen that day and it was hot as hell, no air-conditioning in that room. Sister was trying to sleep, didn't wanna talk, and I was sick from not eating anything but candy bars, so I decided not to stay around any longer. The next morning when we woke up I told her I was leaving and I did. An hour later I was on the road, hitching a ride home. Then Sister showed up, said she'd quit her job and was coming with me. By the next day we were back with Mama and Doc. I don't think she ever left town again.

But all this Mister Fig stuff wore me out. I had to conserve my energy—so afterwards we went to our respective areas; her to the piano, me and Mot upstairs for a nap. Him on the floor, me on the bed. When I wake up for dinner, he's not there. He's downstairs eating waffles again. She made 'em this time. None for me, thanks. I needed out of there, told her I was taking Mot to the movies. She wants to know how we gonna get there? We're gonna walk, I tell her. And she wasn't invited.

I thought I might of seen it before, but I was wrong. It was the title that fooled me. Out front it said THE DRILL INSTRUCTOR, which should have been a war movie. I love a war movie, but this wasn't that. The box office lady was asleep when we came in, so at least it was free. Except for me and Mot, nobody in the back row, almost had the place to ourselves.

It was about a bunch of guys who dress up like women on the weekend. Some place up North, near a lake. What they did was cook and swim in female bathing attire. Splashed and laughed and jumped around telling each other about their ideals in high voices. Come on, gals, soup's on! And they all dash back up to this cottage to eat. The drill instructor part was because of the exercises they did. Bill, the big tough one who knew how to handle himself, was the drill instructor. But his weekend name was Olive. His job was to get everybody in shape to fight the lunkheads from town who had plans to burn down Camp Blanka. Camp Blanka is what they called this place. Also it was the name of their little black bulldog who ate at the table, had his own chair, and was treated like a baby. Then there was some songs. "She's Looking Lovely Tonight" was one of 'em. It was so terrible you couldn't stop watching. But really it was about Olive getting everybody in shape in time to handle what they were up against or they'd all be burned and killed. On the weekdays one was a bank teller, one was a truck driver, and there was a traffic cop too. None of it made much sense. Going about their regular business in town and keeping how they act on the weekend a secret. I think it was supposed to be funny.

They cooked and sewed, giggled and wore earrings together. No women; the only women were them. A couple of 'em had wives back in town, but nothing to speak of. For sure it wasn't a porno film, but at one point a couple of 'em did get into a wrestling match and their dresses got hiked up, showing their hairy thighs, both of 'em wearing leopard-skin jockstraps. If there'd been more audience, likely that would of got a laugh. But Mot got excited, he started slapping his thigh. I nudged him to stop, but he didn't; I had to grab his hand, but then he starts doing it with the other one. Knowing he wasn't capable of doing two things at once

I decide to go up and get him some candy. There was no proper snack bar, but they had a machine. I got him a box of Black Crows and a pack of Neccos, one for each hand. I was only gone just for a minute, but when I got back he wasn't there. There was two exits, so he must of gone out the one when I came in the other.

But no Mot in the lobby. I go outside; no Mot in the street. The box office lady is still asleep. The men's is the only place he could be unless he went in the ladies'. But he's not in either. Nobody is. It didn't make sense. I go back in the movie, look on the floor in case he's hiding under a seat. But he's too big to hide under a seat. Only other place he could be is around behind the screen, but there is no behind the screen. I go back out on the street. Maybe he's tied up in the trunk of some car already ten miles away. It made me feel sick. I think of going to the police, but it's in the wrong direction. I wanted to go home.

As a rule Sister didn't go to bed before midnight. She'd be up practicing her German, singing at the piano, or knocking around in the kitchen. But she wasn't. The house was quiet, the lights were out. No sign of Mot. I creep upstairs already knowing everything gone wrong was gonna continue that way, and I was right. I could hear 'em before I got there, both of 'em snoring,

Mot must of thought I'd left him and come back on his own, looking for me. Then he got railroaded into Sister's bedroom. Who knows? Never having had one, maybe she was holding him like a baby in there. Whatever it was, it wasn't right. Showed what happens when an older woman drinks gin at night. Mot might be a man in body but he was more like a boy in the rest of him, and I felt like going in there, telling her what I thought. But maybe it was different than what I thought, so not wanting to be a chump in the hallway, I went downstairs to check out the kitchen.

Ice cream was all gone. Unwashed spoons in the sink. She forgot to put the cap back on the Gilbey's. You didn't have to be a detective to see what happened. All this made me wish I had a bike. Not a motorcycle, just a regular two-wheeler so I could take a ride, feel the air on my face. I went out back to relax, clear my mind.

Auto was standing next to the pool, chewing something. I tried to get it out of his mouth but he wouldn't let me. Probably the evening news. I sat down behind him—not a best place to be with a mule. Part of me was wishing he'd kick me in the head and if he did I'd kill him. Grass was wet, but it was good to be on solid ground trying to get a grip on things before going up to bed.

I didn't need a dream to tell me, but that's how it came, that *Mot* spelled backwards is *Tom*. In the dream Tom was a snail with a fine-looking shell, looked like mahogany, but the head and face was Mot, and he was crawling over this woman who in the dream was my wife, looked like my old girlfriend Gaylene but better.

Tom was leaving a trail over her white thigh, making his way up her body. I come out the back door of the house, see Gaylene sunning herself next to the pool, and Auto was there too, in the water watching all this. I don't see Tom the snail, but he sees me. I'm coming across the yard and Auto hollers at me to be careful of Tom. I don't know what he's talking about. And Tom hurries off my wife just in time that I don't catch him crawling on her and he's trying to get out of there, going across the lawn, but I don't see him till he gets crunched under my shoe like a piece of candy and it woke me up.

Next morning when I woke up again, I'm thinking about Sister. Her doing what she did the night before was out of loneliness, out of her need to be somebody important to somebody who might like her. But just because you understand something doesn't mean you have to shake hands with it. I could hear her downstairs singing "Happy Days Are Here Again" in German, making breakfast.

I rolled out of bed and stepped on Mot. He was lying on the floor like he'd been there all night. He was dressed too. I stared at him till he looked at me, and when he did it was the same look he usually had, didn't look any different. Like an idiot. I ask him how come he left the movies last night. There wasn't any answer to that any more than there would have been if I asked him the names of the planets. Instead of saying good morning, what I did was touch him on the head, and he kind of smiled. I think he did; it's hard to tell. He remained on the floor till I came out of the bathroom and took him down to breakfast.

How to keep bread from getting old or what to do if you get bit by a snake, there's a trick for everything if you know what it is. The trick here was to be courteous, stay clear of the issue. I treated her just like I was a good customer in a diner and we started having an okay time, but I could tell it wasn't gonna last.

She asked me how the movie was. I tell her I didn't really get to see it because Mot wandered off and I had to go looking for him. She says he came home and I tell her I know that. We don't say anything for a while, then she says she was trying to teach him how to talk. Said it reminded her of Mama. That was about the dumbest thing I ever heard. Because Mama was like a big black man? I ask her.

No, because at the end, Spencer—the part you weren't here for—Mama couldn't talk any better than him.

I didn't take the bait, got up to clear the table. But then doing the dishes, she brings it up again and I tell her the only thing Mot ever "learned" to do was bark, and already he forgot that. To drive it home, I barked at him. He stared at me like it rang a bell somewhere, but he didn't bark back. Case closed.

But she kept going, said Mot was a lonely soul and

needed a mother. I say, To sleep with? That got a rise out of her, and she called me some names. Sticks and stones. She said I was disgusting.

I was tired of it, so I backed off and changed the subject; I asked her about Gaylene. That was my girlfriend before I went away. I already know what happened to Gaylene because Doc told me, but Sister loved to gossip; I like it too—runs in the family. More or less she said what Doc said. That Gaylene got married, married a football player who became an electrician and a drunk, and they moved away, had three kids. I say, I hope she's having a good time with her little family.

She is.

Well, I could have a good time too, I say.

With who?

Nobody.

That brought us to laughing, first her and then me. Sometimes we could do that like with nobody else and we couldn't stop. Then we looked at Mot looking at us laughing and he didn't have anything to laugh at and that made us laugh harder. We're standing there at the sink doing that when the doorbell rang. Sometimes you just know when there's something bad at the door. Even Mot paid attention. We just froze, stood there waiting to see what would happen. It rang again. Sister whispered, Who is it, Spencer?

How was I supposed to know, but I knew she didn't have callers.

The mailman maybe.

Both of us knew that wasn't true. And how come we were whispering? We didn't have anything to hide. I tippy-toe into the front room, halfway expecting the door to fly open, but whoever it was must of left. I look to see what Sister's doing. She's already going up the stairs, and Mot's right behind her. I peek through the curtain. It was because of the quiet I thought nobody was there, but there was.

You don't see people around here on a hot day wearing dark suits and a tie. I thought he was gonna try the door, but he was bending down to slip something under it. This was no Jehovah's Witness or a salesman, plus he had a black car out on the street waiting for him.

I had a bad sense he knew I was inside. Then he backs away, goes down the steps to the street. He looked at the house again, then gets into the car.

There's another guy behind the wheel. You can tell by the way some people drive away that there's a good chance they'll be back.

The card said C. S. CLECKLEY / CONSULTANT / SANTINO & SONS, PUBLIC RELATIONS. In little black letters at the bottom there was two addresses, one was London, the other Washington, D.C. I knew Sister had no dealings with people like that; for sure I didn't. Made me think of Doc's circumcision story, the idea being, one bad thing follows another. I was right not to answer the door; you need time to consider with something like this.

Turned out to be a long day not being able to leave

the house. I tried to get Sister to walk up the block so I could see if anybody was watching, but she wouldn't do it. After a while we all go upstairs for a nap. I didn't get to sleep a minute before she's in the doorway whispering that there's somebody out front again.

I don't know why she's so scared, it's our house—but enough was enough, so I go down to see what the hell's going on. I peek through the window. Nobody there. I tell her the coast is clear, but she wouldn't come down till I checked out the porch. Fine. I go out on the porch. Look left, look right, then there it is, that black car's parked down at the end of the block.

I whip around to get back in the house and there's Mister Cleckley, sitting on the wicker rocker. Didn't look like a guy who ever played football or shot anybody, not any kind of cop for sure, too quiet and polite, gets to his feet apologizing for surprising me. Only thing I didn't like about him, aside from his being there, was that he kind of acted like a blind man who could really see.

He told me his name, which I already knew, and said he'd been around earlier but come back so he could ask me some questions on something we could help each other on, asked if he could come inside a minute so we could talk. I knew if I said no it was the wrong way to go, he'd think I was hiding something. It was hot and he said he was thirsty, wondered if I might give him a glass of water. I did him one better. How about a lemonade?

Said it pretty loud so Sister could get the picture and Mot wasn't gonna make any noise so I showed him in.

I know he knows I know something's up, but we go ahead like it isn't. I offer him a seat, but before I can get his lemonade he tells me he's looking for a man. An African from somewhere I never heard of, and he's laying out the details. This guy, he called him Colonel Motowi, was doing some business up in New York City and either he had a stroke or got into a jam with people trying to kill him, or both.

Whatever Cleckley was trying to clear up was coming out the opposite, far as I was concerned. Then he takes a photo out of his pocketbook to show me. I give it a look, but not really; didn't wanna get involved.

Cleckley's hard to read, wants to know if there's anybody else in the house. How do I know what kind of technology he might have on his body? Playing it safe I call Sister my aunt, tell him she's sick upstairs and I just come in from Shreveport to lend a hand, then I go get the lemonade, which turns out to be a pitcher of ice tea that Sister made before we went upstairs for that nap we didn't take.

I was getting the notion Cleckley was not what he said he was, but if he wanted to be the smart guy, fine, I'd be the dum-dum, and that's what I acted like. It took about five minutes to tell the story he had on this Motowi, but it felt like an hour. When I was in the kitchen I knew he'd be having a look around, but so would I. Sure enough, out the back window I spotted his wheelman coming out of the tobacco shed. And there's Auto on the other side of the yard, head down, pretending he's eating grass. If these boys thought they were a step ahead, they were wrong.

Getting sociable over the ice tea, which he never touched, I ask him what the C. and S. stand for on the card he left me. First name Clark, middle one Shepster, he says. Quite a snazzy name, I felt like saying but didn't. I let him do the talking.

He tells me this Motowi was known to eat the organs of his enemies. "Enemies of the state" is how he put it. Could have asked what state, but I didn't; I knew it wasn't Wisconsin. That this Motowi personally killed and ate a guy from Denmark for instance, but what knocked the wheels off his wagon was the money he took. Cleckley told me they had a saying over there: You can milk the cow so long as you keep feeding it. And Motowi didn't. I almost told him we had sayings like that over here too, but right then I couldn't think of any.

I ask how much this Motowi got away with. He said more money than could be determined yet. True, Mot had some money in his pants, but not an amount that couldn't be determined yet. And how come Cleckley's telling Joe Blow classified info unless he was feeding me a bill of goods?

According to him, Motowi was wanted for murder, rape, and cannibalism, but this undetermined amount

HAMPTON FANCHER

of money is all Cleckley was interested in. Motowi traveled through international airspace and now he's gotta face justice, he said, but that wasn't his main concern; his job was to get that money back. I was tempted to give him a look, show Cleckley a man who never killed nothing but a bee. But if I did that, chances was he'd say Mot was the man he was looking for.

Over there they called this Motowi the Black Weasel, which in that country translates into a mongoose, a snake killer, he says, then shows me that photo again. Big black guys in photographs, especially in fancy military outfits, look a lot alike, I tell him.

Then he pulls out a short, dark string, looked like a shoelace, had a knot in it. This is from one of his shoes, he says. Mot didn't have shoes, except the ones I gave him, and those laces were white. That put me back in the driver's seat, and I draw attention to my own footwear. Hush Puppies with Velcro bands. No laces. That weakened his case, and he smiled a little. Needing a new idea, he asks me how come I think this Motowi killed so many of his own people. That's something you ask yourself, isn't it? Not myself I don't. Although I was tempted to ask if there was a reward—but you can't go one step further if you can't hold yourself back, and I put a lid on it.

He thanked me for the ice tea and my cooperation, said he was gonna go further south, look around down there. Right. I knew he was coming back, probably with a search warrant. Like Doc used to say, a man who wants to rent a pig is gonna be hard to stop. Till right then I never really understood what that meant.

Cleckley never said how he found me, and I didn't ask. From the start I knew Mot was gonna be trouble; anything worth it usually is. All the bones we got are the same after the skin comes off, but till that happens you can't help but be on your own side. Except these days I had Mot's side to be on too. And I didn't forget that. He was the best friend I ever had.

I whistled all clear and Sister brought Mot down. He even went over and looked out the window. Never saw him do that before. Of course she had questions, some I answered, some I didn't. I thought of those lotto tickets and that business with Big Al up in New York—all along I'd been having the feeling I was being watched, but was pretty sure that Cleckley and his gang weren't part of that.

Even considered a visit to Mister Fig, whose first name turns out to be Ernest, which gave me a little more confidence in him. Sister and me discussed it, but I was in the dark on this matter and still am. A person goes too fast, he can get punished; too slow, the same thing. What I was trying to do is stay somewhere in between. I made sure the doors and windows were locked and we stayed inside.

I rolled the TV away from where it was so no light could get seen through the curtains and we settled in. After sundown Auto sometimes brays a bit—likes to let everybody know he's still there, but he was quiet too.

All of us in full cooperation, but I knew they were coming back, and when they did, if I didn't put Mot where Cleckley wasn't, I might lose him.

I did tell Sister that Cleckley and his gang were looking for some African guy who did in a lot of people, just eradicated 'em. A good word, but nothing Mot ever did. Sis agreed. Asked me how he found me. Never asked, I told her, because if I had of I wouldn't of got a straight answer.

Also didn't tell her about the last thing Motowi did before he hit the road was to tie up a certain number of his enemies on the banks of a river full of crocs. Then him and his cronies sat back sipping ice tea and watched the show. Ice tea is what he said too. Right after I brought it to him. Two and two make four, but it wasn't adding up. Cleckley was not to be trusted. Except for Mot, I never met a man who was. All of 'em are bullshitters, not worth the skin they're made of. I include myself in that deal. Sometimes I'd like nothing more than to shoot myself in the mouth, just blow my asshole head right off the top of my neck.

But even if there was a reward, I don't think I'd wanna give him up for it. I was just curious. And besides, I did figure something out, and once you got a plan in place with a measure of confidence to it you can sleep like a cat, and that's what I did.

Before sunup I get Mot up and we went downstairs. He thought we were gonna have breakfast but there was no time for that. First thing I needed was a good sturdy straw. There was a box of 'em in the kitchen Sister used to use for her root beer floats she didn't drink anymore. Then outside and into the shed for a shovel. Auto was curious, started to follow us out, but I shut the door on him, didn't want him seeing where Mot was gonna be.

Morning was coming, so I was required to do it fast. Dug a hole a few inches wider and a little longer than Mot, about up to my knee. Looked like the start of a grave, but was exactly the opposite.

I tied his hands behind his back, blindfolded him too. Not just so dirt didn't get in his eyes—same principle as covering a cage of birds so they stay calm through the night. I held up a finger even though he couldn't see it and said Stay! just like we did on Doc's roof.

But I had a time getting him to lie down in there. Had to trip him. Then I put the straw in his mouth to breathe through—he tried to eat it and I had to give him a slap to make him understand—and then I started shoveling. Soon's he felt the dirt on him he stopped squirming, and I realized it wasn't just the shot Doc gave him back on the roof that kept him calm, it was his nature.

There's times you gotta give people the stony treatment or they'll walk on you. Never with Mot. One of the things I liked most about him was his ability to go along with things. Most everybody'd got a chip on their shoulder. Not Mot: big shoulders, but no chips.

I think he actually felt good in there. Like bread in

the oven. But I knew I couldn't leave him down there for more than a day. I'd give Cleckley and his boys a tour of the area, if it came to that, show 'em I had nothing to hide, and they'd be on their way.

Sister was up, sitting in the kitchen having her coffee, wanted to know what was going on, where Mot was. I told her I'd put him where Cleckley couldn't find him. Made her nervous talking about Cleckley, she thought he was gone, well he is, but if he comes back I was ready for him, I tell her, and change the subject. We talked dental care. About Mot handling a toothbrush. Either that or stop breathing through his mouth. He had great teeth but his breath wasn't good.

Not being used to the dark in the daytime, we could hear Auto braying in the shed. She wants to know how come he's in there. I tell her he was being punished and when his time was up I'd let him out. She didn't wanna know any more.

I go get ready for what could happen next. Went upstairs for a bath and a shave, then I sit down at Mama's dresser to see what Cleckley would see when he saw me. Like looking out a window looking back at myself, and I looked pretty good. Right then I hear the door of the tobacco shed bang. I go to the window and see Auto got out. He looks up, sees me looking at him. I could tell he'd done something wrong, like snatched Mot's straw and turns out that's exactly what he did.

I go down to save Mot, but before I can get out the back, the doorbell rings. I tell Sister to answer it but she runs upstairs to hide. It's either I go to the front door or go out the back to get Mot out before he suffocates.

I go out the back and there's Cleckley's wheelman standing by what was the hole that Mot was buried in. I say "was" because you could see he got himself out. He was gone. There was a lot of mysteries in this deal, but I think a man who gets himself out of a hole blindfolded with his hands tied behind his back probably has a future in front of him.

The whole thing of it, like most things, was both good and bad. On the one hand, we weren't in any trouble, but on the other, Mot was gone and I was pretty sure he was never coming back. It was a blow we might never get over. Who knows? But the air seemed pretty much cleared up, and Sister felt free to walk the streets again.

I put the TV back where it belonged and we were able to relax, but like I said, there was an empty spot. Then it was the old question of where to go and what comes next. It turned out I was right about Cleckley; he did have electronics on him. Everything I said was recorded, but since I didn't say much there was nothing much they could do except have another crack at me. Which they did. I had to go to Biloxi for that. They even sent a car. The guy who drove it was a local and we stopped for lunch, which was on them. Then in this little office, hardly anything in it except a phone and a desk, Cleckley asks me if I was willing to swear I'd never seen this Motowi before and showed me that photo again. What's the point of swearing to something I never saw? I said, and that was it. But I was glad I went. On the way back I stopped in a shop and bought Sister a dress. It was a toss-up about the size, but I got a good eye; it was a perfect fit. A nice wool dress—even though it was summer she was glad to have it, gave her something to look forward to.

My daddy—not Doc, my real one—I never knew. But he was no dummy. And according to Mama, he had some real talent. Before I was born he taught a cat to walk backwards. That's what she told me, showed me a picture of it, a black-and-white snapshot of a cat. But it's hard to tell in a photo if something is walking backwards. But I believe it was. Once I asked Sister if she thought he really taught a cat to walk backwards. She didn't think so. She thought it was an idea Mama got from watching TV.

I remember those things too. Commercials they had for cat food with this snappy-looking cat walking forwards, then backing away, back and forth, faster and faster. Of course it could of got achieved by a technical trick, but so what? I stood up and tried it, watching myself in the mirror. A few steps forwards, then a few steps back. Faster and faster, I turned it into a little dance.

NARROWING
THE DIVIDE

A white rat is running. Running away from a grim building on a moonless night. Avoiding the gutter, the curb, and the street, he sticks close to the shuttered storefronts. He is terrified, and his destination is vague.

Later he will say, There's a place you can't get to, no matter how fast you go, and I have the feeling it's the same place I'm running from. And Jim will say, Me?

Anybody! Ratty will exclaim. The man will admit he doesn't get it. And Ratty will say, All we can do is try, Jim. And Jim will say, I like it when you call me Big Jim. Me too, Big Jim, Ratty will say. Then Jim will say, Should I kill you now?

But right now, Ratty is in the street. He has no plan, except to get away from where he was and keep it that way. He has a picture in his mind of where he needs to be; he saw it in a magazine. A safe, caring place he never had called home. A double-page spread on shiny paper that he stood on, slept on, on the floor of his cage, which he tried not to shit and piss on. But finally he gave in, the picture was ruined and removed, then replaced with want ads or sometimes the funnies, which he loved. Sooner or later, though, he spoiled them all. But in a kitchen, like the one in the picture, was where he wanted to be.

He is afraid to be alone. He's never been alone, yet he'd rather be alone than with who he was with. The doctors. The other animals.

J. The hope is, is that we get to learn something, and I think I might know what that is.

R. What might that be, Jim?

J. That we shouldn't take any of it seriously.

R. You mean anything that you and I, as in we, have done, and are doing right now or about to do?

J. Anything, anytime, all the time.

R. Jesus, Jim! I mean, Big Jim. That sounds like heaven.

What follows wouldn't have occurred if the rat had stayed behind the base of the sink when Big Jim came in to piss. He didn't know where to run. There were places to hide, he could feel it, but lacked the experience. Jim, standing in the doorway in his socks and underwear, a big man with a hairy belly, almost bald, except for the ponytail.

Ratty leaps, he's flying through the air, so fast Jim doesn't see it, but knows it happened. He heard the splash. Jim slams down the lid. Silence. Ratty up to his chest, holding his breath, peering at the crescent of light that circles the seat. Jim flushes the toilet. Then lifts the lid. Ratty scrambling to keep clear of the thrash and bob of the roiling water.

Faced with the size and menace of the man, Ratty shrinks back, his little mouth quivering, trying to form sounds. Not squeaks, but words, English words.

J. What?!

R. I know I don't belong here, but I got no place else to go.

Jim's scowling down at the white, pink-eyed Ratty, the nails of his paws scratching at the slippery porcelain.

R. Would you give me a hand, please?

No, Jim is not about to do that.

R. Right.

J. How come you can talk?

R. Can I call you Jim?

J. How come you know my name?

R. Because before she went to bed I heard your wife say it—your name. Heard you say hers too. Those are good names. Penny and Jim. The answer to your question, Jim—can I call you Big Jim?

J. Why?

R. I don't know, it just seems right. Okay! I'll tell you. I'm a lab rat. *Was* a lab rat. Lots of things I had to learn. Talking was one of 'em, for whatever good it did me.

Ratty loved to talk, couldn't help it, even in his sleep. One might say he'd been wired for it. Indeed he had been. In the lab they did a lot of that. It makes Jim nervous talking to a rat, but he'd be a fool to forego what might be an opportunity. "Big Jim and his talking rat"? Although he won't think of that till later, whereas Ratty is already thinking ahead.

For Ratty there is the possibility that Jim could be a sanctuary, at least an accommodation, if he plays it right. And Ratty is fast, it is his only strength, but one thing he knows is not to make the mistake of impudence. It's gotten him into trouble before. It's already clear that he's an object of disgust.

R. Lots of things I had to learn. Learned to talk, tried to master penmanship, the old Palmer method. I love them all, but I can't do 'em. You pick up a pencil without a thought, Jim. That would be deliverance for me. I can pick one up, but can't use it to write . . .

Ratty has just leveraged himself out of the toilet. He lands on the floor, shakes himself off. Jim steps back, repulsed. Ratty looks up, ready to collaborate.

R. I miss being an animal.

J. You are an animal.

R. Not a pure animal. I been compromised. If I hadn't learned to talk, I wouldn't be ashamed. I'd be what I was, be what I'd been, if the lab hadn't of got me. No guilt, no shame. Like Popeye.

J. What?

R. Never guilty 'cause he never does anything wrong.

J. You're not making sense.

R. I'm too nervous to formulate, Jim. It's the language, trying to understand each other, the chimera of interpretation.

J. The what?

R. When I was a rat—

J. You're still a rat.

R.—if I ran away from something I wasn't a coward, I was just a rat running from something.

Ratty glances at the door. Jim pushes it shut.

R. How smart does a rat have to be before killing him constitutes murder?

J. Murder?

Ratty senses the advantage, but a touch of defiance is needed.

R. That's right, pal, murder. Is that what this is coming to?

Jim is not sure what it's coming to, he's not on solid ground.

R. Feels like we could be on the brink of something important here, Big Jim.

And maybe they were, but neither of them understood exactly what it was. Yet each felt the excitement, the promise of it. Ratty more than Jim. Ratty has done a lot of reading. In the lab library he gleaned information on the history of his kind and in hopes of impressing his host:

R. They can scale vertical walls with no surface to purchase, swim nonstop for six to ten miles, tread water for three to four days, gnaw through lead pipes and cinder blocks . . .

J. Who do you mean, "they"?

R. I mean, we, us, them, me! Exert twenty-four hundred pounds of pressure per square inch in each of our teeth. Plus the willpower to shut the lid on temptation if it puts us at risk.

He waits for a comment, but Jim offers him nothing.

R. In 1946, when a team of scientists surveyed the island of Dumi Bardo in the South Pacific for the effects of radiation caused by the atomic bomb, they found it to be the only creature surviving. The rat, I mean. The island abounded with them; none were maimed or genetically deformed. Those guys were in top shape. Robust is how they put it. Thriving.

Facts like these gave R-63YU, informally known as Ratty, the courage, the confidence, to escape, and from that unlovely building where he was imprisoned and trained, on a warm moonless night, he set out to change his fate. But Jim is no pushover.

J. So how did they live, these atomic rats of Dumi Bardo? Ate each other?

R. Good question, Jim. Take my case, for instance. What did I eat? I didn't, is what. Starved myself.

J. Why should it make a difference to me if you did or you didn't?

R. Because it goes to the heart of the whole predicament. I'm talking about the tetrachlorodibenzodioxin they slipped in my bowl. But who ate it? Not me. No sir, in preparation for my big escape, I didn't eat for a week.

Ratty pauses for breath, has to gather his thoughts, assess how things are going, knows he'll have to be prudent, but his nerves won't cooperate. He's malnourished, confused; his ideas keep jumping the track.

R. Alien intruders is the last thing you need around here. I know, I'm not your problem, Jim. But for me it's either back to the lab or the gutter. I won't be a burden to you, I swear. Maybe I can even help you out a little.

J. Help me out a little with what?

R. Solidarity! Collaboration and the benefits of doubt—pluralism is the water that puts out the fires of dogma.

Suddenly Ratty falls to the floor, rolls around squealing, holding his head. Comes out of it twitching, disoriented, backs away from Jim. Jim's never seen a rat slam out.

J. You don't have rabies, do you?

R. God no, that's a dog disease.

J. Yeah, and they get it from rodents.

R. Mole rats, maybe, reckless squirrels. I'll be okay.

J. You want some water?

R. No! No water! Don't put the water on me! Ask me another question. First thing that comes to mind. Help straighten me out.

Jim just stares at him, doesn't ask anything.

R. Probably lots of people don't think this, but sometimes I do . . .

J. Do what?

R. Think that people, some people, don't like rats because they don't like themselves.

J. What the hell would anybody think that for?

R. Because rats and people have a lot in common. We're the only two animals that attack and kill their own kind. An alligator doesn't give a shit about his kids, but a rat does, he makes a good father, looks after his own. Just like a man.

J. Okay, I'll give you a question—you ever been chased by a cat?

R. Thankfully no. Never seen one. But I've seen pictures . . . You don't have one, do you?

J. I hate cats.

R. Right. That's great. I understand. Not an animal that inspires trust, the cat. Dogs, on the other hand . . .

J. Never mind about dogs.

R. Natural selection weeds out the incapable, Jim. The useless cat will be extinct in another few years. Dogs are another matter, they're useful, noble.

Ratty didn't have to be told that Jim was a professional dog man; he figured this out from a photo he found in the garage. A publicity shot. Jim in an anorak and goggles surrounded by an assortment of dogs, and over his head in print it said BIG JIM AND HIS DANGEROUS DOGS.

R. I could tell you were some kind of performer. You're tall and good-looking enough.

J. Had my own act. Traveled the country.

R. Wow! Bet you did. What kind of act was it?

J. Wild dog show.

R. Oh, my, that must have been something.

J. It wasn't your standard dog act. Not just dogs jumping through hoops and walkin' on their heinies.

R. You mean these were smart dogs.

J. These dogs were mean. Had bad tempers. I had to work 'em in the cage. Nothing people love better than a man with a wild animal act.

R. I can see you must have been popular—nothing people love better than a wild animal act. What happened to it?

J. My lead dog died and I got married.

R. A mature decision, a man has to consider his wife, Jim. Probably you're better off for it. Dogs can make trouble, chasing cars, biting people.

J. Rats bite people.

R. They don't chase cars. White ones don't bite people. Unless you sit on one. You could be in the presence of a rat without even knowing it. When you guys have a war, for instance? There's an inflation in the rat population. Lot of action at the seaports, poultry markets, slaughterhouses. Did you know that?

J. For a rat you know a lot of stuff.

R. It's all in the books, Jim.

J. How the hell you turn the pages?

R. No can do, but that's a good question, Jim! It's because of the keyboard; I'm hot with the keys. I grant you, before the computer revolution a rat that could read was a rarity. For the most part, in fact, it still is.

You take a brown rat, he can't read shit. But you try and smack one with a stick? And he's cornered? He'll be going up your arm, then down, tear the nails right out of your fingers! But us little white rats, we're harmless, we're a horse of a different tail—I mean color! You know what I mean?

J. I don't know why you're telling me all this . . .

R. Hold on, I'm not done yet. Now, brown rats are mean rats and the black ones are worse. We're dipping into a contentious subject here, Jim. Animal awareness versus human perception. The insects, the amoebas—who knows? On the one glove you got the ones who think animals can't think, but on the other? You got the ones who are saying they do—making up situations to prove it. Controlled situations, behavior modification. Fucking anecdotes! They tried to kill me. You were doing it too, Jim.

J. I don't think I could kill you now.

R. Maybe if I went in there and jumped on Penny's eyes you could. Eh?

Ratty just made Jim laugh. Ratty's never heard Jim laugh; Ratty laughs too. Jim's never heard Ratty laugh; makes him laugh harder. They laugh so hard they run out of breath to laugh with. Then silence. Jim goes thoughtful.

J. I love my wife. I love my wife more than I love myself.

R. That's good, Jim.

J. How would you know? My wife is sick.

R. You're right. I mean, how would I know? What's wrong with her?

J. None of your business.

R. I've been in love. Once. Once with a doctor and once with a rat.

J. That's twice.

R. She bit me.

J. The doctor or the rat?

R. Right here. Look. The rat. She was a dwarf.

J. The doctor?

R. No, the rat. The doctor was a full-grown woman. Vicki, big Jewish girl. Smart, smart as hell, but boy, she was mean. Trying to overturn the stone of consciousness, see what's underneath it—she probed me, Jim!

J. You mean up your—

R. No, no, up here, my brain! Stuck needles in my head!

J. Shhhh! You're gonna wake up my wife.

R. Sorry! I just want you to know, whatever you decide to do with me can't be worse than what's already been done.

J. Okay, okay, calm down, I'm not doing anything. Have I done anything?

R. You threatened me!

J. That was an hour ago. Forget it.

R. I'm trying, but I almost died. You were gonna flush me down the toilet!

J. What the hell were you doing in there?

R. You know exactly what I was doing in there!

Besides, I was thirsty, trying to get a drink, okay? (He's yelling again.) Sorry!

J. I thought you said . . .

R. I know, water's funny that way.

J. Come on.

Ratty follows Jim into the kitchen, watches him get down a bottle of whiskey, a glass, and a saucer. Jim fills the saucer with water, sets it on the floor. Ratty has a sniff, then laps it up. Jim watches, sips his whiskey.

R. Why can't I have what you're having?

J. You can.

Jim pours whiskey into Ratty's dish and Ratty laps that up.

R. You're a prince, Jim. That hit the spot, twenty pellets in the bank of health. A palliative to a sickly rat.

J. So, what about nurse what's-her-name?

R. Vicki? Doctor Methley got her. I seen it happen. Tied her up by the hands with a red scarf and had sex with her.

J. You mean, raped her?

R. No, it was her idea. Never mind about that. Let's hear about the dogs.

J. They're gone. I told you.

R. Get new ones.

J. I don't want new dogs.

R. Then let's hear about the old ones.

Jim doesn't wanna talk about it. Ratty scoots closer, as if he did. Jim has a closer look.

J. You got toenails like banjo picks, you should get 'em clipped.

Ratty stares at his toenails. He doesn't get it. Looks up at Big Jim.

R. Are you being mean to me?

J. No! Just saying what I see.

R. Come on, Jim. Let's hear the story. Please?

J. Okay, thing was, I was on the road a lot, so had to give it up when I got married. The best way to do things was her way. You know what I mean?

R. Sure. Somebody's got to be the boss. (He looks at his toes.) I couldn't climb so good if my nails were clipped.

A sudden clanging from the other room. Ratty jumps.

R. What was that?!

J. Alarm clock. She was on a diet. Very strict schedule.

R. I'm not good with bells.

J. It'll stop in a second.

R. But she shouldn't see me, right?

J. No. She doesn't like rats. Animals, in fact.

R. I guess that explains the dogs.

Jim pours him more whiskey and one for himself.

R. Maybe you could get another one, a dog I mean. Start over. Is that a good idea?

J. Not like Dan. There's not another dog in the world like Dan. We had a special routine, one of a kind.

R. Tell me.

J. These dogs were hard to work with. There's a lot of tricks they wouldn't do, commands they wouldn't obey. I trained 'em that way. I kept 'em wild and vicious, get in there with as many as ten of the meanest dogs anybody ever saw. Dobies, Rhodesian razorbacks, bulldogs. A seventy-nine-pound cocker spaniel.

R. That's a pretty big cocker, Jim.

J. Brown was so fat he could hardly move. But if you got too close, he'd rip your balls off.

R. Christ, what kind of tricks could you do with a dog like that?

J. Kick him, till he got mad enough to chase me, then I'd put Dan on him. Soon's he felt Dan's teeth in his neck, he'd lay down. Always got a big hand on that one.

R. Sounds like a real nice show, Jim.

J. The beaners loved it.

R. You and your dogs. It's the story of stories.

J. It's not a story. It happened. Married a woman who hated dogs. I'll tell you one thing, you know right where you stand when it comes to a dog. A dog won't call you names. If he does, you could kill him and nobody'd give a shit. Law of the Yukon.

R. The catchy item in your story there, Big Jim, is that, ah, well, the betrayal of your talent. Right? I've had experience with this. Gnaw your way through one wall, and whoa, there's another one! You ever read any L. Ron Hubbard?

HAMPTON FANCHER

Jim shakes his head.

R. No problem, you're better off for it—hold on to your purity. What about the so-called rule of parsimony? You familiar with that?

J. Okay, what's "parsimony"?

R. Exactly! Basically it's the simpleminded orthodoxy that posits an injunction against attributing human traits to animals. If that isn't a crock, what is? There's nothing alive that doesn't have to wrestle with a pressing problem—even a beetle's gotta reflect. If he didn't, how could he find the dung?

J. Relax.

R. Sure! Good idea. You got good ideas. We'll table this stuff for later—I like talking to you. You want me to go under the couch and sleep? Am I starting to make errors?

J. You're doing fine.

R. Maybe it's okay to have a problem. "I'm okay, you're okay"—we got a problem? Wouldn't be alive if we didn't, right?

J. Only the dead don't have problems, is that what you're saying?

R. But we don't want to die.

J. That's the problem.

R. I think we cleared something up here, Big Jim. Trying to be meaningful and significant makes us feel like shit. *Die Menschen zusammen unter der Stille!*

J. Jesus, you speak German?

R. No! Yes! "Humans together under the quiet." Only

the dead cooperate. You don't have to be a German to understand that. I saw a crocodile tear off a monkey's arm!

J. Hold on, Ratty . . .

Ratty suddenly tears around in a little blur of a circle. Jim jumps out of the way, watches him swerve and turn, then fall over, panting.

J. You okay?

It takes Ratty a couple of moments to recover. Dazed, he gets up off the floor. Stumbles over to Jim's big foot and sits down next to it. Jim wants to move, but doesn't. Ratty's eyes, like a little child's, look up at Jim's.

R. What did you say?

J. I said, you okay?

R. You're my best friend, Jim.

Jim moves away. Ratty falls asleep. Jim stands there contemplating him. Then, exhausted, sits, rests his head on the table. He notices an ant, mashes it with his thumb. Another one appears over the edge. He lets that one live. It's quiet in there for twelve hours. Jim can't tell if he slept or not. If he did, he dreamed Penny either went shopping or to church. Ratty wakes up and goes at it:

R. Shopping, eh? You know what a research rat is worth in the defense department budget? Eight bucks! That's right, and who gives a damn? I'll tell you who! The animal rights people, who are doing what for who?

Nothing for rats! They're going to bat for the canaries! What's so special about them? They can't even talk! A parrot I could understand.

J. I don't think they do experiments with parrots.

R. That's right, because they're mean and they're funny. What do parakeets do?

J. Canaries.

R. Right, excuse me. Dying in coal mines is all they're good for. The lion is courage, the bull is strength.

He laps what's left of the whiskey in the dish.

R. And there's the famous snake in the paradise story and the white whale in the other book, but where the hell is the parakeet—I mean canary! Between medical and so-called scientific, not to mention cosmetic, research, more than sixty million animals a year are murdered—dogs, monkeys, and rats mainly. The liberals are hiring lawyers for the dogs and the monkeys, but who's going to bat for the rats?

J. You know anything about baseball?

R. What? No, I don't give a rat's ass about baseball. See, there's another one: The ass of the rat is worthless, but a leg of lamb costs money.

J. That's because people eat lambs.

R. Not Hitler, he was a vegetarian. He admired the mystics. Places in India where rats are worshipped. *Rats* spelled backwards is *star*.

J. There's been some monkey stars. I don't know about rats. Mickey Mouse, maybe.

R. He's not a rat. He's not even real. You can't trust something that's not real. A rat you can trust, but you can't trust a monkey. They'll go on a rampage. That monkey in the Tarzan series? He lives in Palm Springs, spends his time watching reruns, eating Doritos, and drinking lemonade.

J. Fuck the monkey.

R. Right. What's the worse thing she ever said to you?

J. Who?

R. Accused you of. Penny.

J. Lately? Hasn't accused me of anything.

R. She must of told you something.

J. She told me I took the joy out of living.

R. That's a hell of a note.

J. Yeah, but she had a sweet streak too. Had a weakness for kids. Used to be a retarded boy lived down the street, an idiot who she'd let come over, let him watch her water the lawn, teach him how to count, give him a cookie if he could go to ten.

R. What happened to him?

J. Committed an error. Got ahold of a match and started a fire. Lost his visiting privileges.

R. Poor kid.

J. Pissed him off. He'd come over, right up to the edge of the yard, and scream at her.

R. Scream what at her?

J. *Fire lady!* Then he'd swear at her until she got fed up, had to put the hose on him.

R. I guess he had it coming.

J. Wasn't his fault. He didn't know what he was doing.

R. Did you go to bat for him?

J. Sure. No.

R. Sure? No? Which is it? It's okay, I see what you mean—what's the point, huh? Maybe I should get out of here.

J. No, no, it's okay. She'll stay in bed.

R. Cynophobia is what the white-coats call it. Fear of dogs.

J. She also had fear of comets.

R. Cometophobia, eh?

J. Penny would never go out of her way to watch a comet. But if she heard a dog howl or bark and imagined a comet streak across the sky at the same time, she might go mad. At least that's what she said. And syphilis. A syphilitic dog could kill her.

R. Sweet Jesus, do dogs get that?

J. I don't know. Mine never did. I just know she had a fear of it.

R. I can't help noticing you refer to Penny a lot in the past tense, Jim. Right? Would I be wrong?

Jim drops his head, stares at the floor. Ratty waits. Jim whispers:

J. I poisoned her.

R. Ah! I knew something was up. She didn't smell it?

J. Nope.

R. Peanut butter?

J. Meat.

R. Wow! Put it in her meat. What kind of meat, Jim?

J. Don't want to talk about it. You hungry?

R. Not as hungry as I was. I'd like to have a nice little turkey carved out of a block of wood standing on one leg.

J. You like art?

R. Yeah, I like the ads. I like reading 'em, seeing 'em.

J. Lies is what they are.

R. Yeah, but underneath 'em there's secrets to be found. Right?

J. Secrets are bullshit. Get 'em off your chest and there's still something wrong.

R. Sounds like you been through it, Jim. That's why you're cynical. Me too.

J. You got secrets?

R. They hot-wired my head, fucked with my brains, doped, poisoned, electrocuted, forced me to do unspeakables; I was locked up, made to fight, teased, frozen, starved, and driven nuts. I'm trying to recover. That's why I came here.

J. That's not your secret.

R. I'm trying to make friends with you so you don't kill me. But I also kind of wish you would.

J. I'd kind of like to, but now I can't.

Over the stove the plaster Christ on a wooden cross is what Ratty is looking at.

J. That's Penny's.

R. I figured. I'm no expert, but I've looked into that story, and I just don't get it. I mean, where's the salvation if the Savior dies for love? Or anything else, for that matter. Love kills, is that what that is?

J. You gotta be willing to sacrifice for love, is what that is.

R. Ah! Yeah, I see, okay. The dogs. Right? You made the sacrifice, Jim. If love was easy, everybody would be doing it.

J. If love was easy, it wouldn't be love.

R. My God, you're right. If love was easy, it wouldn't be love. Are you mad at me, Jim?

J. It's customary to be mad at rats. But no, I'm not.

Ratty gives it a respectful moment.

R. You're a man to be admired. You had a secret, you disclosed it. What that is, is trust. They could bash out my teeth with a rock and I wouldn't talk.

J. Who's "they"?

R. Just a figure of speech. But it's deeper than that. It's like I'm your own creation now, your very own little white rat who knows what's in your heart.

J. The heart, just a damned muscle. It's a blood pump.

R. You know what I mean. This is like a beginning. Like the first day of creation.

J. There was no first day of creation.

R. The beginning, then.

J. No beginning, no end, that's just the way we think.

R. Keep teaching me, Jim.

J. Okay, rat, you understand that now is not the same as then, right?

R. Couldn't you call me Ratty, like you did before?

J. No reverse gear in the transmission of time. It's gone, like an ash that used to be a tree. Ratty. Okay?

R. What's gone, the tree?

J. I'm saying everything goes from more to less; more is what's gone.

R. More or less of what?

J. Sense.

R. The older it gets, the more sense it makes?

J. And the less sense it makes, because everything increases. You see? Stupidity, intelligence, space, time, birth, death. The new stuff sits down on the old stuff. The old stuff gets squeezed out.

R. So if you're older and more, you make less sense?

J. Try to pay attention.

R. I am!

J. The Gorves increase, but not the Dowlves.

Ratty squints at Jim.

J. There's always something new that wasn't there before, and the more there is of that, the less there is of the other.

R. The other being what used to be. What was. The Dowlves. The squeeze-outs?

J. You got it. That's as simple as it gets. The more organized the system is, the more confusing it becomes. The perfect confusion is what the universe aspires to be. And you know what stops it from getting there?

R. The Gorves?

J. Don't fuck with me.

R. I'm not, I'm trying to . . . Okay, you say each and every thing is not really real, because all it can ever be is how we see it. Which is the Gorves, a shape based on how we see it?

J. Has nothing to do with it! Gorves don't have a shape.

R. But the Dowlves do—is that right?

J. No! It's not. You don't know shit about the Dowlves.

R. I'm trying, Jim. But this stuff is hard.

Jim shakes his head. It is hard.

R. Come on, don't give up on me, we're just getting started.

Jim has a drink.

R. I love the way you drink.

Jim pours a little more into Ratty's dish.

R. So, you were saying, irreversible . . .

Jim nails Ratty with a look.

J. What is?

On the spot, Ratty, doe-eyed.

R. Cosmic evolution?

J. Here's what happens. The system fails because it can't survive what's outside it.

R. So what's outside it? The system.

A shrewd and telling grin from Jim. Ratty notices his mentor's eyes are crossed.

R. You mean death?

J. Ha! Death is nothing compared to what's outside it. Death is predictable as dirt, in a uniform. But what's outside it . . .

Ratty waits. Ratty can't wait.

R. Don't mean to be a pest, Jim, but what's outside it?

J. Not the Gorves and the Dowlves. We know what they are. You see where this is headed?

R. You may as well kill me.

J. It won't make a difference. Not anywhere is where it's headed. There is nowhere to go. There is no *go*. *Go* doesn't mean anything.

R. So what does?

J. *Stay*. It's the most important thing ever said: *Stay!* It's one thing we can never do.

R. That makes sense.

J. No, it doesn't. It never will.

R. You're smart, Jim. Excuse me.

Ratty finishes off his saucer.

J. I took a course in engineering, but I couldn't cut the math.

R. But I bet you do the crosswords, right?

J. My fallback was the dogs. Yeah, sometimes I do.

R. That's why you're so good with the words.

Jim fixes Ratty with a look.

J. You know what it means to rat on somebody?

R. Snitch on 'em, like Judas did to Christ?

J. He ratted him out.

R. I get it, but rats don't do that.

J. It's the rat who leaves the sinking ship.

R. Be a fool not to.

J. I smell a rat. What about that?

R. If you think I might not be reliable or loyal, you would be wrong. You could've kept this business about Penny to yourself if you really didn't trust me.

Jim looks away, stares at the wall.

R. Maybe we should go outside, sit in the garden.

J. We don't have a garden.

R. Looks like a garden.

J. It's just grass. Let's have another drink.

But Jim doesn't move; he's gone grim, just stares at the wall.

R. Snap out of it, Jim! We were talking about the heart, remember? Not the muscle, like you said, but that it's big and wants to help.

J. Help who do what?

R. Help us understand how come we're misunderstood!

J. You understand why you're misunderstood, then what?

R. Then you don't blame somebody else for it.

J. Somebody comes up behind you, hits you in the head with a hammer. You say, how come you did that? Whatever the answer is, two to one, it's bullshit.

R. That's philosophy, Jim—go on!

J. Then there's the physithurisms.

R. What are those? Physithurisms.

J. The sound that the leaves make in the trees, in the breeze. But the parasites and the coffin flies make a sound too. Put 'em in a paper sack and pop it, have it for lunch. Or they have you. Then there's the other school of thought; save yourself so you can save something better. Which is like putting an armchair in your grave. Either way.

R. Lay down your life for a better Mexico?

J. This isn't Mexico.

R. It isn't?

J. No, it isn't.

R. Did it used to be?

J. Everything used to be something it isn't. Like a grasshopper in a cup of coffee. No matter how good it is to make a plan, it's always better when it's canceled.

R. That makes sense.

J. No, it doesn't.

At any second, Jim could have yelled *Knock it off!* and that would have been that. But he didn't, and now Ratty wants to kiss him, but lacks the lips, and if that weren't the case, he still wouldn't kiss him because Big Jim wouldn't allow it.

There is half an eggplant on the counter, a bowl of sugar Ratty sampled before he was caught, and two unwashed dishes in the sink. This is not the kitchen of his dreams.

Jim had counseled him to take none of it seriously. Yet Jim was struggling to set it straight. The Gorves and the Dowlves. Ratty wasn't born yesterday; he knew there were no such things. Keep drinking and pretend to teach is the thing. Ratty and Jim, narrowing the divide.

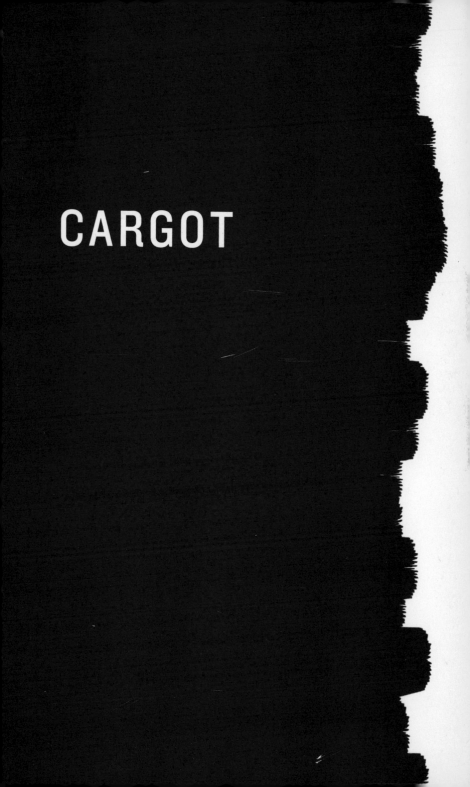

CARGOT

changed my name again. Last night I decided on a new one, a name that will stick. Cargot. Not like *got*; the last syllable should be pronounced like *go*, the French way, *Car-got*. A name to accommodate a big load of talent. No first name, just an initial. They'll say, What's the S for? Sam? Nope, guess again. And they might, but they won't get it, and I won't say it. That's it, I'm not going to change anything about myself again.

Lots of days and too many nights dreaming about what needed to be done, and now I'm doing it. Way back when he was big, I knew Troy Donahue. That's when I got the bug, but for some reason, fear maybe, I avoided the risk of actually taking the plunge, of making the commitment. I remember one day, Troy brought his agent over for a barbecue, a lawn party, not unlike this one I'm about to attend, and I had a chance, the chance to make an impression, but I was shy, I felt ugly, insecure, and I blew it. That agent died a long time ago, he got fatter and fatter and then he was dead. And now I hear Troy is gone, but I'm still here, and today I come out of my shell.

There comes a time when talent, no matter how much it's repressed, must come forth and claim its place with those others, the greats who've preceded me. I know it's a journey, but no matter what the obstructions that rise up before me, I'll get around them, over them, plow right through them if need be. It's a question of tenacity. No matter how high the peaks, the steaming swamps, the flat arid deserts, the insurmountables, I'll reach the goal. An actor worth his salt is a pilgrim to Mecca. (I don't like salt.)

O cunning Love! with tears thou keep'st me blind / Lest eyes well-seeing thy foul faults should find. Shakespeare! *Yes, I have tricks in my pocket, I have things up my sleeve. But I am the opposite of a stage magician.* Williams! I love Tennessee. I've worked on them all and read everything that's come my way. The mystery of that radiant clarity that occurs when the inner identity of a thing shines forth and is about to break out of it's shell. I go forth. *To find in motion what is lost in space—*that's Tennessee again, God bless him.

In the past I was accused of being indecisive, fussy. My capacity to vacillate was boundless. I would suffer disaffection at the drop of a shoe. Labile as a douser's pendant, my coach used to say. He had the words. Pronounced *lay-bile.* I looked it up. But the slippery defect of my virtue was paranoia. Nothing clinical, of course, but if you persist in being disappointed in yourself for being unable to do the impossible you run the risk of becoming your own worst enemy, of devolving into something small, or driving into a lamppost. I don't want to think about it.

To be multi-amphibian is the thing, to live in many worlds at once. Ambition. I was afraid of it, or used to be. I was obsessive, I admit it, but an actor should be. I told my coach what he was teaching me was starting to feel like a wall between what I was and what I needed to be, and he told me to get out. I felt like a blind man on a roller coaster. At first.

I couldn't even afford a place to live, so I stayed in the big garage. Agent Barkus used it as a gym, at least part of it, but he never worked out, so he let me sleep there till I got on my feet. His wife, Gloria, has an SUV. Barkus has a Lexus, but for a while, there was room for me.

I used to live in a world of hypotheticals. If such-and-such happens, will the outcome be a benefit or a setback? But no more *to-be-or-not-to-be*. Action is all. *Whoso divineth upon conjectures may as well shoot too far as too short.* Too much thought and not enough doing is bad for the actor. But *I run before my horse to market*. Let me speak for here and now.

I'd seen it before, these Saturday afternoon get-togethers. I knew what to expect; flirty money worshippers drinking Pinot Grigio around the pool, getting up and sitting down. Squalor is what I call it. And if you refuse to convert your attention to the schemes and irrelevancies of their material concerns, you go unnoticed. That's the respect that makes cowards of us all.

Not me; I aim to remain solid, but supple, the optimal state for an artist. Money means nothing to me. I'm as poor as Jesus.

I don't have much party cred and I'm no crasher, but invited or not, I'm making my move, managing my route in such a way as not to be seen.

The grass feels sharp, newly cut, maybe it's not Saturday—this must've been a gardening day. Trying to keep a cool eye on things, but I got to admit, I'm nervous, overheated. But screw it, he cast me out and now I'm back. Here to show Emperor Barkus that he's got no clothes. Here to have my way with his wife.

He'd give me advice and shirts he never wore or got tired of. And sometimes, if he had a beer or two, showing off for his buddies, he'd tell me to recite some Shakespeare. Just short little pieces—he didn't have the patience for more. It made me feel like a whore. See how I rhyme things?

The path is quiet and green. Shimmering blue of the pool, like a Hockney. No birds in the birdbath. Generally animals are not attracted to Barkus. Even his dog didn't trust him. With good reason. I make my way across the yard. Beach towel spread on the grass. In her white bikini, no top. She has oiled herself. She shines.

Feels like I've had a dose of actomyosin, whatever that is, whatever it is that's making my muscles contract and expand. Excitement, I guess. I'm trying to be nimble, but it's a struggle. I've decided if today I succeed it means I'll play the Dane. Not yet, but eventually I will, and in a brand-new way. I'm going to do it as a Mexican aristocrat, Old California. A Zorro-type Hamlet with a sword and a whip, and when Barkus gets the news that I'm in a hit he'll pull out what's left of his hair for not believing in me in the first place. I hear music coming from the house, but don't feel it, not like I once did. No need to hear music anymore; I feel constructed of it. Her body, closer now, makes me fizz.

Back when I lived here, I tried once and she made fun of me. Didn't even tell Barkus. Or so she said, but she must have because when Barkus tried to sell me on the hot dog stand, he accused me of it. He took me to the car wash so he could get his clean Lexus even cleaner. Barkus could never get clean. He owned the place, or so he said, the hot dog stand as well. He wanted me to buy it, said I could pay as I go. I told him I'm not a hot dog vender, I'm an actor. I should have a fallback, his wife was worried about me, then he says, I know you're fucking her. I told him I wasn't. I wasn't. I don't think he thought I was either. Just give me a down payment, he says, borrow it from Gloria. I sign it over, you hire somebody who knows what he's doing, doesn't mean he has to know much. Put a wiener on the grill, mustard on the bun, and you're in business. He thought that was funny, he laughed, trying to disparage me. He would like me to trade my dream in on a hot dog stand. If ever I play Mephistopheles in *Faust* I'll know who to model it on.

The Devil is a gentleman / he dances very neat / wears patent-leather shoes on his pointy little feet . . . That's not Kit Marlowe, of course, but it fits, except Barkus has big stupid feet and footwear to match. He wears customized cowboy boots with fancy stitched dancing girls riding on the backs of wild-eyed longhorns made of hand-tooled fossilized eagle claws and kangaroo hide. He told me you had to have a license to wear them. Three grand a pair. His initials, W.B. (first name is Walter), engraved in white rhinestones at the top. Loud too—he's got taps on the heels. Truth was he didn't give a shit about the Old West, but he fancied himself some kind of gentleman cowboy. The only gentile to run a major agency in this town. Have your Jews call my Jews, he used to say. I heard him do it once, then he winked at me.

I've come from behind the hedge, from the raw and unruly into the refined, faultlessly crossed the grounds under the burning sun, but I must be early. She's out to get some rays before the party starts. Or do I have the wrong day? I'm confused.

Who knows what it all means, how things happen. Suddenly you just end up somewhere. You take the journey. Who was it, Pauline Kael, said Hollywood is the only town where you can die of encouragement? I hadn't been encouraged in a long time. I wouldn't mind a little dose of that kind of dying.

The sun is so swanky even the shadows shine. Up close every blade of grass is crystalliferous, but the

　　　　　　　　　　　　HAMPTON FANCHER

distance is blurred, I'm nearsighted. I can make out the outline of two persons on the porch, one short and fat—that's gotta be my friend, the humble gardener, José—listening to the instructions of King Barkus. If I don't hurry, my duet could turn into a trio, even a quartet, but from the look of the lawn, I think José is done for the day.

I try to remember that people are odd and more fascinating than starfish. Miscellaneous points of kindness. Even Barkus had his loyalties. Not to Maxwell he didn't. Mainly to money. Maxwell was the dog. But I do have mixed feelings. Exasperating and selfish as he was, I had a soft spot for Barkus. He liked to take a walk after dinner, for instance. When I realized it wasn't for the fellowship of sharing a stroll beneath the stars, but to stimulate his bowels, I liked him even more. I admire a clever agent. He relaxes not to calm himself, but to be coiled and ready for the next deal. And sometimes he reminded me of a fat little boy, the way he laughed and clapped his hands when he was happy. I could understand how Gloria loved him. But it's a question of space I would think—people only have so much room to care about something else beside themselves.

Maxwell wasn't a purebred, but he wasn't a mutt. Usually the mutt is small; Max was built like a wolf. And he was smart too, more like a person, but better. He could have been a star back when dog movies were big. Maybe that's what bothered Barkus—not making money off him, but his agency didn't rep pets. One night he tells me, get rid of Maxwell. Take him somewhere, drop him off, and drive away. Where?

I don't give a shit, he says, just get rid of him. I was dumbfounded. If you can't do this one little thing for me, how do you expect I'm going to do anything for you?

He was talking about my career.

He wanted me to drive him to the desert, Newhall or someplace, push him out of the car. There was no way would I do that. I'd just take him down to Sunset, let him out there. For sure he'd get picked up by some babe in a Lincoln; the ladies loved Maxwell. But it didn't happen that way. Going down the hill we had an accident. And that was the last I ever saw of Max. I don't remember the details, blindsided I guess, but it must've been bad. I don't like to think about it, but I'm pretty sure that's when everything changed.

It happened sometime around then; I can't recall exactly, there was no face to it, just a memorandum slipped under the door. It said the gym was going to get expanded and that was that. I was out. José told me they were going to tear it down, the garage, but not so far they haven't. Before me, Barkus had another actor who lived here. A sadder story than my own.

I saw a photo of him. He was a raw, handsome young man. Some said if he didn't drink himself to death he'd be the next Jimmy Dean. But instead, on Christmas Eve he drove his Austin-Healey off a cliff. That's how come I got to live here. And for a Hollywood minute, which is about three or four months, Barkus talked like I was going be a star. One of those short-lived enigmas who flame out fast and become legends, I guess. Who knows? But I was never fast, never caught fire. Never even drank.

I admit, there is vengeance in this enterprise, but the tune of it is love. Not for her, but for the work itself, which is everything. *The Prowling Pilgrim* is a musical I'm planning to write, going to star in it too. Already I've got the first line to the opening song: "Dead birds in standing water don't fly away so fast, / because the Almighty ain't strong enough to make the future last." Self-reliance is the theme. Destination? Broadway.

We all need attention to embellish ourselves. To suffer the setbacks without losing heart is the thing. When I wasn't working for Barkus, I studied the Bard. Oh, those words! But living a life of double-duty hyphenated me. Who was I? How is it I got like I am? That kind of thing. But the greats must be defiant in their willingness to be misunderstood. To persist when no hope can help and none is offered. I didn't even have a phone. Barkus was too cheap to install one. That actor who lived here before me, the one who drove off the cliff, was a dirty lodger. The area around my bunk stunk of bacon and nicotine, and opening the window didn't help. If I complained Barkus made fun of me, called me Mr. Sensitive. In the innermost meat of his being, what actor is not?

Here's what I call a correlation: How come we're

fascinated by what we abhor? For fear of its power and the good it could do us. He's a major agent, no way around it, but I was never even an official client, no standing at all. His fancy friends, they all knew I lived in the garage. That I had no phone. But what about Gloria? She was a call girl before she met him. Not a streetwalker—she was high class—but still, what right did she have to look down on me?

Her foot! The pedicured toes, the polished nails. I'll cover the length of her before this is done. It's a tricky situation, though; if she wakes, what then? But it's not like she was always snooty to me. More than once, going to market or bringing in the mail, I got the sly look from her, I swear. Now here I am to claim the crown! Joking. Here to claim what? Not sure exactly. But great journeys are not for the cautious; still, distances have to be gauged. I'm not going back to check, but I think it was her knee I just passed.

"I can't breathe, come away and see me!" is what I dreamed she would say. She never did. But I know one thing, I'm no longer on standby, I've made my move.

But progress dresses in setbacks, we all know that. Something could go wrong, and I've never been good at what happens next; I must stay alert. Gloria's muscular and stuck-up, proud that she's not fat. Already I'm conveying myself along the ridge of her thigh. I'm moving fast.

Rarely was I ever invited into the house for dinner, the parties and all that. Actually just once, the day before Christmas, for an eggnog and a gift. White socks. I kept them for a while, but never wore the things. I can't bear wool on my skin.

The upper thigh is achieved. I'm startled by something dark next to me. It's my shadow! More time has passed than I thought. I have arrived at the juncture. The eternal triangle, this *nest of spicery*, a little box of treasure to unlock. But *mar not the thing that cannot be amended*. Not that Gloria is a virgin, but what a glorious line! And as if on cue, I hear the cry of a passing bird, a crow I think. The *vile squealing of the wry-necked fife*. There's some bardolatry for you!

Paradoxically, in sleep, she welcomes me. Our pulses are in sync. I travel the firm soft roof of her tummy, the ticking organs beneath the skin; I can feel the angel energy of her blood thrumming through me. I am a silent tide on the heedless sea of Barkus's wife. Onward! I climb higher, extend my neck to look again. Beyond the sprawl of the yard, there's Barkus on the porch still talking to poor José, who is wearing a newspaper on his head like a pirate's hat. It's too far away to hear, but I bet the topic is a wage cut. If Barkus turned now he would see me on her breast.

The tissue of her nipple is like the skin of myself, no contradiction. For some reason I feel like crying. The idea that she would take me in I gave up a long time ago, but the dream of love does not punch a clock. The head is where I'm headed, her face is slightly tilted, the profile sublime, the golden clutter of her hair a crown. But I'm not so good of a sudden. Something flits and flutters within me. I feel wobbly, my balance is off. Could be sunblock. She's probably slathered with the stuff. *O tiger's heart wrapped in a woman's hide.* Always a reckoning to be paid.

In the hollow of her clavicle I pause for breath. Here is a spot the color of coffee, the size of a tear, her birthmark. *But it delights not me.* This project is done.

I climb to the knob of her shoulder and try to adhere. It's hard; I feel sleepy and sick. An association with me on top is what I came to achieve and I did!

To mark the occasion a little more Shakespeare would be good, but there's no time. Barkus can be brutal when he's upset. I need traction. He comes! Above all, I can't afford to take a fall. But the strumpet awakens—I go!

A relief to be on solid ground. But here's the stupid part: I've taken a tumble, landed on my back. Barkus is bigger than I thought. Now the bottom of his boot, the silver half-moon of the tap nailed to his heel, as am I, transfigured in the grass. For a moment I saw the sky.

DEAD MAN
FLYING

He didn't have a choice. Ignog needed the job; he was on his knees. So broke he had to sell his dead father's cuff links to buy a ticket from LAX to Seattle and back. The Sisters of Vindictive Mockery had its headquarters up there.

Ignog would rather have done it on the phone, but Lazard wanted a face-to-face. It was Lazard who had given him his first job, given him his name, in fact. Ignog was not his original name, but Lazard deemed it a compelling byline, and you didn't argue with Lazard.

The Sisters of Vindictive Mockery was a monthly of critical discourse, politics, literature, and art, but it was the interviews, interviews with famous people who were famous for never doing interviews, that made the magazine. J. Paul Getty, Cagney, James Jesus Angleton (almost), J. D. Salinger, General Franco the week before he died, Madame Chiang Kai-shek at the age of ninety-nine. Ignog got to her through the laundry man.

He had done four years at the Sisters and six covers (a record), but the more he excelled, the less he was liked, plus he was slow. After taking seven months to turn in "The Imperial Dogma of Top-Down Doctrinal Pedophilia, War and Foot-Washing," an anticleric screed of two thousand words, he was taken to a last supper at a café called the Pickle and fired. Out of indignation, Ignog snapped back with a book. An underhanded investigation on why NFL running backs who happen to be handsome tend to succeed, but before dying, usually of sclerosis of the liver, raised children who were losers and brats. It was his first and last book. Not a big seller, but it was well reviewed and led to higher ground. *Harper's, Esquire, The New Yorker.* The good stuff. Then things got bad. And Ignog did the bad stuff. Then no stuff. He hadn't worked in over a year.

He thought a lot about calling Lazard, but Lazard was mean and Ignog's pride was frail. Then, out of the blue, Lazard called him. The assignment was to interview one of the richest and most inaccessible eccentrics of the twentieth century. An old-school tycoon who loved money, airplanes, and big-breasted starlets. When he was alive, Howard was a household name, revered and feared, and now he was dead for thirty-eight years.

Kleenex. Howard was famous for his obsession with it. Lazard thought Ignog should call a shrink, get a medical opinion. A shrink would cost money. Make it up then, read a book. Ask him what he thought about 9/11. Who, the shrink? No, Howard! Write down what I'm saying. I'll remember it. No you won't. Lazard punched him on the shoulder. Write it down! Ignog started scribbling.

Find out why he stopped tying his shoes. Ignog figured it might have been the accident back in '47. After that Howard knew he wasn't invincible, lost his edge, stopped changing his clothes, didn't shave or cut his hair. Lazard wanted Ignog to interview people who thought it couldn't be done. What couldn't be done? All the things he did, the shit he invented when he was young. The wrenches, drills, whatever they're called—oil-sucking devices. And talk to his enemies, dig into his origins. You want me to go to Texas? No! Lazard didn't want Ignog to go to Texas. He wanted him to buy a bottle of Listerine. You smell like booze. On second thought, never mind the Listerine, do it on the phone. Lazard was rich but cheap. He had to be. But what he didn't want was stale, hashed-over, already told, dickhead facts. Unauthenticated, sensationalistic conjecture from unreliable sources would be fine. And he didn't give a damn about lawsuits either.

That was one of the advantages in interviewing a dead man. But the estate still had lawyers who could make money litigating posthumous claims. Fuck the lawyers. Here's a wacko who lived on a mattress in the middle of a hotel room surrounded by memos he wrote to Jane Russell's tits. But maybe you got a point, Ignog, the fucker ran a movie studio, he bought a city—get an explanation for that. Write down what I'm saying! I already did. And don't forget the beard. Went to his belly, right? Right. He never washed. So full of phobias he wouldn't let anybody touch him. Wouldn't touch himself. Never wiped his ass, is what Lazard heard. Had bugs in his hair. Lived on burgers and chocolate bars. Common knowledge, but Ignog wrote it down. As far as he knew, there had never been a successful interview with a dead man. Lazard said the Mormons were setting it up.

Bugs in his hair and his biggest fear was public opinion! Can you beat that? Ignog tried, told Lazard he had found out that the Spruce Goose was really made out of cedar. You sure? He said that if it didn't fly he was gonna leave the country. But it did fly. For seventy-two seconds. Right, then he locked himself away, shut the door. Richest man in the country died of starvation. He watched *Ice Station Zebra* a hundred and seventeen times, Ignog offered. Not to be outdone, Lazard said the man wrote over one hundred memos regarding Jane Russell's tits. Write it down. I already did. Fine. Clover Field, Santa Monica. Tomorrow at midnight. Be there. Lazard gave him a hundred dollars and Ignog caught the eight o'clock back to L.A.

Ignog was nervous; he didn't have a plan, an approach. Usually dying didn't work well for people, but for Howard it was different, and maybe that was an angle a journalist could use. This is more or less what Ignog was thinking as he waited on the tarmac at Clover Field at midnight the next day.

He saw it before he heard it. Two lights, then a third, in the sky, blinking yellow at the tip of each wing and winking white at the tail. It came in smooth and loud, hit the runway, ran to the end, turned, and taxied back to where Ignog was standing. The twin Pratt & Whitney radial engines suddenly got louder, then diminished to a thrum. Ignog stood there staring at it, an Abbott 71—cute, but butch, like a two-headed bulldog, low slung. The cockpit was at eye level, too dark to see the pilot clearly, but Ignog knew who it was.

A hatch slipped open. Ignog turned around and carefully backed into the opening. The bulkheads vibrated as the engines revved, the Bulldog swiveled, sprinted down the runway and into the sky, headed for the Pacific.

Howard had been in the air, been in the Bulldog, for thirty-eight years. Whatever it was that kept the tank full and the oil pumping crapped out about once every seven months. Seemed to happen when there was an eclipse or some other celestial irregularity. These things irked him, but south of the border, he had his special places. This time he was north, this time it was Clover Field, not far from his old plant. But the Bulldog needed no maintenance; he had come down to pick up a journalist.

Howard wanted a burger. His functionaries were well paid and followed orders. He tapped the memos out in Morse code over the two-way with the long nail of his left index finger. This journalist would come aboard, hopefully with a burger. But the idiot didn't have one. Howard wondered whose fault it was and fought back a tantrum. He couldn't eat anyway, just wanted to touch it, a sniff maybe, then toss it out the window.

Ignog belted himself into the copilot chair. At a hundred feet and climbing, Howard introduced a subject, a test really: the Napoleon complex. He wanted to know Ignog's definition of it. A little man compensating for being small by acting big? Bingo. And what was it about Napoleon that made him so enticing to the inmates of loony bins? Ignog suspected it might be an invention of the movies, something to do with the outfit, especially the hat. He hoped that Howard liked that answer. Howard coughed. Encouraged, Ignog speculated that there were probably a lot more people who thought they were Jesus or Howard than Napoleon. He couldn't tell if Howard was flattered or wasn't; the man was not easy to read.

Approaching Catalina, a second question: Why did Ignog come into the plane backwards? It wasn't voluntary; Ignog was suffering the first stages of Parkinson's. Howard already knew this, but he wanted to hear Ignog admit it. He was glad to know somebody who walked backwards. Occasionally he did it himself, but didn't want it to be official. Was it random coincidence that pilot and passenger shared a disease, or was it fate? If the former, who would profit by it? If the latter, how could sympathy be avoided or exploited? It irritated Howard to be uncertain on this.

At least the passenger was a tidy fellow. Howard was not, but they weighed the same. Ignog was balding and small, Howard hairy and tall. Ignog's head barely reached the top of the back of the seat. The crown of Howard's narrow head touched the roof.

Catalina approaching. The Bulldog flew over the northern tip of the island, then back again, circled. Howard said they couldn't be seen, but they were there, below in the scrubland, eleven goats. Too dark to see, but Ignog took his word for it. Bill Grogan, a long-gone second cousin, had owned the old Catalina narrow-gauge railroad, Howard said, and the goats, back then, when there used to be more, were a hazard to the train. There was no train anymore, just those eleven goats were left, the mangy offspring of the originals. Interesting. And the Bulldog climbed.

Look behind you. Ignog did. He had already noted the clutter of jars full of yellowish liquid. He guessed it was just a way to get things started. You're here to continue my moment, Ignog, and it better not be a question. I don't take questions.

I would rather listen to a burro, a rooster, a sheep, scream in the slaughterhouse than the human voice, so address me without talking, write your questions on that pad you just got out of your pants.

Ignog's teeth chattered. It's cold in the Bulldog. A

thin, two-buttoned coat and slacks aren't enough. But Howard isn't even wearing a shirt; just an old leather aviator jacket, unzipped, no pants. A wing-tip shoe on one foot, the other one bare.

Write down what you have to say, Ignog, then read it to yourself to make sure you got it right, then read it out loud to me. Understood? Ignog started to reply, but caught himself. He wrote *YES* on the pad, then pretended to read it to himself. Read it, Ignog! Ignog did. Ignog read it to himself, then said, Yes, understood. Okay, Ignog, let's get started. On the pad, Ignog wrote, *I have a tape recorder,* and then read what he just wrote, then spoke what he just read. Let's see it. He handed Howard the tape recorder. Howard had a quick look, dropped it, and stomped on it.

Watch this. Howard lifted his other foot, the shoeless one, to show Ignog a trick he could do with his toes. He crossed each toe, starting with the little toe, over the next toe, all the way to the big toe, without using his hands. How do you like that? Ignog was impressed and started to write. Just say it! I thought you didn't want me to talk. It can't be helped—and speak up, I'm hard of hearing.

Ignog asked his first official question: Is it true you can't turn on a light without first washing your hands? Of course it's not true. That's ridiculous. Did you just challenge me, Ignog? Simple question, Howard. Howard was silent, he wanted to think about this. He had to wash his hands before he turned on the lights—it was true. A thorough washing, both hands wrestling in the slippery wet soap, in the dark. No reason to turn on lights in the daylight. The idea of having to turn on the lights in a place without a place to first wash his hands made him nervous. So far it hadn't happened, but how would he manage if it did? One option was not to turn on the lights, remain in the dark till sunrise, or just not be in such a place. But why should he bother to explain this to Ignog?

Tell me, Ignog, are you honest? Yes, Howard, I am. Do I smell? Yeah, you do. Do I care? I guess you don't. You guess?! Do you know why I don't? Why you don't care, or why you smell? The latter. Because you haven't had a bath in twenty-six years?

It was phew city in the Bulldog. The cockpit smelled like cat piss. But if this was the price of admission, it felt like a bargain to Ignog.

Howard wanted to talk about surveillance and identity cards; he thought darkies, chinks, and beaners were victims who would turn on their betters if they were not kept an eye on. Howard didn't trust anything or anybody who wasn't Howard. He was an intolerant, overdeveloped excluder. Ignog was passive, underdeveloped, and excluded, and even in childhood could not abide intolerance or prejudice; yet here they were, flying through the night, their bodies almost touching, surrounded by Kleenex. A pilot and a copilot who couldn't fly. But they both believed zealots of unconditional loyalties were wrecking the world. A crocodile and a gecko together in the sky, if they are not upset, have something to agree on. And Howard mumbled a story to Ignog about Nevada Smith, the only friend he ever had. Nevada had an older sister, long dead, who was briefly married to Bill Grogan—the man Howard had called his cousin? Interesting. But the subject seemed to darken his mood, and Howard was silent again. But not the Pratts; the cockpit was noisy.

Now Ignog noticed another sound, a thin, piercing whistle—no wonder it was so cold, there was a little hole, the kind an incoming bullet would make, a sharp-petaled crown like a distended aluminum anus, next to the trim tab handle just above him.

Howard hoped Ignog would ask how he navigated, but he didn't. By the clouds, Ignog. What? Never mind. Howard and the Bulldog liked engaging clouds. There was a nice one a mile ahead, chalk on a blackboard, shaped like a reclining lady. The Bulldog suddenly banked and dove, tearing a hole through the middle of her. Howard screamed Wilko! and was nice again.

Were you surprised when they attacked us, Ignog? When who attacked us? You know who! We been sticking it to 'em since the pacification of Mesopotamia. And considering I'm part aviation and part skyscraper, I must know something about it—isn't that what Lazard told you? Tricky Howard, always a step ahead. You mean the Twin Towers? The Twin Synagogues is what I call 'em. If our enemies won't bend, we break 'em. That's how it's done. Finally they get fed up, retaliate, and we scream "Foul!" send in the troops, drop the bombs, and occupy. You know why? Why? Because we like to, that's why. I don't. Of course you don't, but the question is, how can you prevent it? I don't know, Howard, what's the answer? The answer is not to acquire bizarro clients in the first place, because when everybody gets to the second place we gotta go over there and kill 'em. (Great stuff, Lazard would have to admit it, Ignog was coming home with the bacon.) Remember Watergate? Of course. I had that man in my pocket, Ignog. Then he turned into a frog. You can quote me on that. You're talking about Tricky Dick? He wasn't so tricky; all he wanted was more money. He tried to make a deal with the Devil.

Ignog didn't believe in the Devil. The Devil is the one with the money, Ignog. You can't come by much of it without him. Howard had once gone to a midnight event where the Devil spoke. The Devil told the audience that he hated his horns. An old millionaire in the first row asked how it was that he got 'em. The Devil said he needed a distinguishing feature. The back of his head was flattish and sloped. That too. And the goatee? A line of logic that started with his feet.

You're not a Hebrew, are you, Ignog? Ignog wasn't, but he had abiding admiration for Jews. The Devil's playground is the monkey bars of guilt and pity, Ignog; either you fly or you fall. There's nobody that won't let you down. Not a system in the universe that won't finally fail, at least the Jews know that. But the Bull-dog will never let you down. Then Howard gobbled like a turkey and accelerated straight up into an in-verted loop. Ignog felt weightless at the apex, apogee, or whatever it's called, then they retroflexed, diving straight down. The port engine flared fire, the Bulldog snarled and rolled over into a corkscrew. Ignog sang a high C.

But Howard was one of the greatest pilots who ever lived, and since he was dead, how could he die? What was there to be afraid of? By and large, the man invented modern aviation—all the old hands knew it; he was bet-ter than Lindbergh, Rickenbacker, Amelia Earhart, and Yeager combined.

In his research Ignog found out that, blindfolded, Howard had once executed forty-eight touch-and-goes, landings, and takeoffs consecutively (one for every state in the Union) and had only crashed once, back in '47. He got banged up pretty badly, but it wasn't his fault.

I could never make enough to be repaid for what I've lost, Ignog. Nobody can. You probably think that "love" could do it, but you would be wrong. I didn't say a thing, Ignog almost said, but didn't; he knew Howard already knew he almost had.

Socratic irony was Howard's weapon of choice, and Ignog could put it to good use. This thing would write itself. Lazard would love it. Starting with the laminated

Rules of Conduct next to the bullet hole, riveted to the bulkhead.

a. English only.
b. Never touch the pilot or the Bulldog's controls.
c. Behave well in turbulence; vomiters will be ejected.
d. Adjust your dress before leaving.

You familiar with the experience of not being able to make up your mind? Ignog was. Howard held up his left hand. On the one hand I think about cutting them, but on the other I want to see how long they'll grow. He was referring to his nails. Ignog didn't want to look. It was a recurring nightmare about a witch he had as a child. Henry, for that was his name when he was young, would find himself in the dead of night hunkered on the floor of his mother's closet. He would feel a breath of cold air on his back and look up. The roof of the closet had opened like a trapdoor, and in the stormy sky above hovered a hag on a broom. Henry scrambled to get away, but with a shriek, the rod of her arm whooshed down and grabbed him by the neck. Her long-nailed fingers so tight around his throat he couldn't scream. Then, like a fish on the hook of her hand, he was yanked off the floor and hauled into the night.

Now I'm gonna tell you *my* dream. And Howard made

a buzzing sound. You hear that? Ignog did. Okay, the fly is loose! Free, can go anywhere, do anything it wants. Buzzzzzzzz! I'm the richest man in the world. That's not true, Howard. Who's richer? According to *Schollup's Book of the World's Richest*, you were twenty-second. Only in the United States were you the richest. Or used to be. Howard cackled. I killed a lot of flies! Look in the glove compartment. Ignog did. Look at those pictures. Ignog did. They were drawings of flies. No, they're not, they're photos. They didn't look like photos. A page of pictures, pictures of flies engaged in valiant, mischievous, supportive, meddling, aspiring, interceding, collaborative activities. They look like drawings, Howard. They're photos, Ignog. Who took them? Robert the Hungarian. Ignog hadn't heard of him. He was that daring rascal who caught the death of that Republican soldier with his Enfield flung back behind him coming down that hillside in the Spanish Civil War. This was before poor Bob got creamed by a Commie land mine in Vietnam. He wrote me a letter. You know what it said? Two words: *Terra Incognita*. Can you beat that? It's pretty good, Howard. What do you think it means? Other than foretelling his death? I think he was referring to you. You're a smart boy, Ignog. Would you go to the cleaners for me? I'd be glad to. That's good to know, Ignog.

But Howard changed his mind; he wasn't ready for the cleaners. What he wanted was a sponge bath. Ignog wouldn't do it. Howard wasn't used to being denied—it

HAMPTON FANCHER

hurt. And Howard couldn't hide it. It's nothing personal, I just can't do it. Howard could understand it, but
still, it hurt. He sulked. Perhaps this was a good time to
ask a sensitive question. How come he never had any
children? What makes you think I haven't? Because no
legitimate offspring have ever come forth to make any
claims on your estate. Would you like to be that offspring, Ignog? Have me instruct a sum of money into
your little mouse of an account? Of course you would.
But what about something better, Ignog? Would you
like to take a ride in the Goose? Sure you would. Are
you serious, Howard? No. Well, maybe. We'll see.

I Howard was an expert at the upper hand. But Ignog
had some tricks of his own. You piss in those jars, right?
That's why you keep the Kleenex around. That's not
why! You drink it? I ask the questions. And no, I don't
drink it. Is that what they think?

I don't know what they think, Howard, but some
people say it's a remedy. Who says it's a remedy? The
Aztecs. Fuck the Aztecs. A remedy for what? Their ail-
ments. I save it. For what? You're never gonna know the
answer to that, Ignog. I'm good with that. Howard
didn't like Ignog saying he was good with that. And
don't call me Howard. You think I care if they ridicule
me? They tried to get me on that Watergate thing, but I
can't be gotten. That was a long time ago, Howard. Up
here nothing's a long time ago! And you're never gonna
fly in the Goose, Ignog. Whatever you say, Howard.
Don't call me Howard!

They're in awe of you, Mr. Hughes. Howard wasn't assuaged; he closed his eyes, dropped his head, letting go of the controls. The Bulldog tilted, went into a dive. The only thing Ignog ever flew was a kite, but he grabbed the yoke. Howard shoved him away. Don't ever do that!

Ignog needed to untie the knots in his stomach, but the plane was doing things that were making him sick. Vengeful Howard was pushing the Bulldog into transonic deeds. Ignog's eardrums felt like water balloons. He leaned forward, tried to put his head on his knees. We're going to China! Ignog said nothing. I took you for a man who was game to go. Ignog said nothing.

Are there two people in this plane, or just me? I'm right here, Howard. Prove it. The Bulldog settled down. Ignog lifted his head, looked at Howard. What about Jane Russell's tits? What about 'em? Why were they so important to you? What makes you think they were? The memos. They sold tickets those tits. And Howard almost smiled. The world sits up for a secret, Ignog. Breaking the sound barrier was the last great thing that ever happened. That stupid moon landing was a gyp, a witch on a broom would have been better. So, breaking the sound barrier made Howard happy. It wasn't me who broke it, it was Yeager, and it's not about "happy"! Being on top is what winds the clock, Ignog. Reach me one of those boxes back there.

Howard's Kleenex. To get at it, Ignog had to unbuckle. Soon as he popped the clip on his safety belt, his door flew open. A two-hundred-mile-an-hour wind whipped in. Fifty Kleenex boxes sped out into the night. Close it! Ignog is trying to, struggling to keep from being sucked out himself. Howard grabs him by the neck, strangling him. Ignog wrestles the door shut. You're a cocky little wacko, Ignog! Wasn't my fault, Howard! You wanna blame the plane?! I didn't do it. Yeah, blame the plane, but if you hadn't been here, it wouldn't have happened! If you say so, Howard. Don't call me Howard! Three-quarters of my Kleenex, gone! He figured Howard must have a secret button that opened the door. If so, he just tried to kill him. But also rescued him.

Not to despair, Ignog, one of the thieves was saved. But don't presume, either; one of the thieves was damned. And on top of it the bastard sounded like a Saint Augustine fan. Whatever he was, it would be good for the article.

Nothing wrong with being a coward, Ignog. You can't help it. That Howard made him for a coward wasn't fair. He wanted to ask him to explain, but he didn't. Howard explained anyway. You're up here acting like this is an interview, but it isn't. You don't have a clue and you know it. What you're hoping is that if we ever land I'm gonna give you some money, more money than you could otherwise have. What do you mean *if* we land? I mean I don't think you really want to. I want to, Howard. It's too late, Ignog. Shall we sing?

Ignog was shocked to realize the Bulldog seemed to

be flying itself and shocked again when he noticed that Howard had an erection. You and I never learned to enjoy ourselves, but to go flying over China at night is gonna change all that. We're gonna find joy, Ignog. Shall we sing?

I'm not much of a singer, Howard. Let's give it a try. You know "Bill Grogan's Goat"? No, I don't, I'm sorry. Don't be, just pay attention. Howard leaned closer and sang. Bill Grogan's goat was feeling fine. He ate three shirts from off the line. Bill took a stick, gave him a whack, and tied him to the railroad track. The whistle blew, the train drew near. Bill Grogan's goat was doomed to die. Howard suddenly stopped singing. What do you think, Ignog? The goat gets hit by the train? Wrong. There's one more line. Howard sang it softly: Bill Grogan's goat coughed up the shirts and flagged the trainnnn.

Pretty good, eh? Yeah, it's great, Howard. You know what it means, Ignog? That if things are about to go wrong, you can change them? Good try, Ignog, but that's not what it means. That if you steal a man's shirt, you're gonna pay the price? Have you made any money, Ignog? A little, but not your kind of money, Howard. Not many have. There should be an Olympics for making my kind of money.

Howard flew high and hard. Ignog was getting used to it. That sinking feeling had diminished. Now it was the anticipation of being returned to the ground that felt like dread. *Terra Incognita.*

Flying with Howard was something like no thing, not future or past, not actual or otherwise, but more dream, like an odalisque chambered in a night that would never end.

A little while longer, that's all any of you have. A little while longer? That's right, Ignog. You want more? What more is there? Up here there's more than down there. Down there it's depravity and death; I bought a city of it. Up here it's the venerable customs of the air. Which are? Inscrutability. The world has become an unmysterious place, Ignog, a Vegas. But the sky is endless, rhapsodic. Grounded you submit, but up here . . .

Before Howard could finish the sentence, the Bulldog sputtered. Oh, my. What? Quiet! Is something wrong? Ignog watches Howard fiddle the choke, crank the flaps. Both men groan as the Bulldog silently descends.

THE CRAB'S
WELCOME

The name tag on her tunic read OLYMPIA. Three desolate blocks in Red Hook was her route. She pushed her cart up the empty sidewalk and stopped in front of a four-story tenement across the street from Abe's warehouse.

Before he came to the window to watch her, Abe was in the bathroom checking his neck. He suffered from a swelling of the lymph nodes, something akin to scrofula, the nurse at the clinic said. It wasn't as bad as it looked, didn't hurt much, but the blistering was unattractive and he didn't like being at the window when there was a flare-up.

Not that the mail lady would notice; she was across the street sorting the mail. So far Abe had never exchanged a word with her, never had the occasion to. But the Kid across the street did; he was sure of that.

Abe did his talking at the window, saying what he would say if he ever got the chance.

I'm grander than you, more glorious, and if I decide you're worth it, long-legged mail lady, I'll paint you with fire. You'll never be able to spend the wealth of my love, not in a dozen years, a dozen lifetimes!

Abe was an artist, a small beaky man, lean and

fervent—at least at a distance. He even wrote her a letter once that he never sent, but couldn't find.

Everybody on the block hopes you're smart enough to take advantage of me as soon as possible. I'm taller than you . . .

He was not taller than her. Olympia was almost six feet; Abe wasn't quite five-six. And he didn't know anybody on the block, made it his business not to.

He watched her go up the stairs into the tenement where the Kid lived.

What happens to the small apartment of a seldom seen father and an untidy Kid was the shape this one was in. The Kid was sprawled on the couch, one foot cocked on the cushion, the other on the floor.

He was puggish, quick-eyed, and ten. Bottle of beer in one hand, letter in the other; what he was reading was making him wince:

> *You have been selected by a higher being. You're the kind of woman who needs to have it put to her forcefully.*

Jeeez, give me a break!

> *I'll make you roll over on your back, show me your soft parts. To one such as you, my science is magic.*

You wish!

*I'll tickle and lap your succulent vitals. The
effects of my desire will ripple like moonlight
on the pond of your flesh . . .*

The Kid stuffed the letter back in the envelope, finished his beer, and got to his feet.

Abe was looking for a needle to sew a button on his
pants when he was jolted by the knock. He froze, he
waited. Whoever it was knocked again. There was
nothing to do but go to the door. Abe did, opened it,
and there was the Kid, holding up the letter. Abe didn't
know what to do. The Kid said:
    Take it.
    What is it?
    A letter.
    So?
    You send it?
    To who?
    Me! It was in my mailbox.
    Abe took the letter, and as soon as he did, he real-
ized he forgot to put on his pants.
    Read it.
    Abe extracted it from the envelope, pretended to
read a couple lines.
    Where did you get this nonsense?

I told you, in my mailbox.

The mail lady must've made a mistake.

There's no stamp on the envelope.

Like I said, she made a mistake.

Maybe. Maybe not.

There were people on the block who knew what Abe did, but nobody the Kid knew had ever been inside the warehouse. Abe could see the Kid was curious and stepped aside to give him a look.

He'd watched the Kid for more than a year, knew some things about his life, had gone through his trash. The Kid had watched Abe as well, seen him have an argument with a tramp once about an umbrella that Abe said was his.

The Kid slipped into the warehouse. Except for a cot and a trestle table bearing the tubes, cans, and brushes, all the wild slop of the painter's trade, the place was almost empty. But there were lots of paintings, some leaned against the wall, some were hung, all of them portraits, except for one. A dirigible grounded on a barren field. The Kid fixed on it. Abe watched him move up for a closer look.

You drink with the mail lady? I see her go into your building, I don't see her come out.

What is this, a blimp?

Yeah. What color eyes she got?

How would I know?

Brown, right?

Hazel.

Which is about the same thing.

There's green in brown when it's hazel.

You know your colors, Kid. How come you don't go to school?

I go. I just don't go outta my way to do it.

Abe didn't know any kids, never had one look at any of his paintings.

What are you gonna do when you grow up?

Interview the Crab Man.

You watch the show?

Of course.

You think it's gonna run till you grow up?

Doesn't have to. Crab Man's about to retire.

You drink with her, right? I see her go in, but I don't see her come out.

Sure you do. You see her come out. I've seen you looking.

You have sex with her?

I'm ten.

Brush up against her?

Once.

Her against you, or you against her?

Abe could see the Kid had no interest in this line of thought, so he got to the point.

I wanna paint her.

The Kid held up a thumb and squinted at the blimp like an artist appraising a perspective.

I like this blimp.

Abe watched him turn away, make for the exit. Not

right letting him leave without saying good-bye, but "good-bye" wasn't right.

You like the Crab Man more than you like yourself?

No. I like myself more. But I like myself more because I like the Crab Man.

Then he went right for the door, turned back to Abe, sliced the air with the flat of his hand, and left. Abe walked over to the blimp to have a look for himself.

I like myself less than I like this blimp, which is why the blimp makes me feel good about myself. I guess that's about the same thing.

For dinner the Kid had boiled weenies and made himself a cocktail of vodka and pineapple juice. This was a special night. The apartment was dark except for the TV. He sat on the floor in front of it, illuminated by *The Buster Pleasely Show.* Buster was interviewing the Crab Man.

Engirdled in his amber shell, the Crab Man was all crab, except for his little flat face, which was locked in a frown. One of his eyes was missing, but his claws were large and handsome; they dangled over the box he squatted on.

Jolly Buster was a large bald man, impersonator of wide-eyed sympathy, but he had no use for anybody and the audience loved him for it. He looked up from an index card.

I have a question here from a fan in the audience: Is

it true *The Crab's Welcome* was originally conceived of as a daytime kiddie show?

The Crab Man didn't like the question.

Let me tell you something, Pleasely, and the hairball halibut jawhead who wrote that question—

Please, no need to be formal, call me Buster.

I'll call you Cluster! I told this already on *Larry King*. The network didn't believe the nation was gonna embrace a crustacean. And they didn't—kitty show, pussy show, or the hamsters they rode in on; not till I started writing my own lines did *The Crab's Welcome* become a hit.

The Kid scooted closer to the screen. Pleasely stoked the Crab:

So you shut down the morning show and turned on the night, thereby snapping up the ratings. I see!

Then see if you can't get me that bowl of salt water I asked for in the green room that nobody brought me yet.

Sorry! Bowl of salt water for our guest, please!

I'll throw it in your face!

The audience roared. The Crab Man rattled his claws. The Kid took a gulp of his highball. Buster kept rolling:

But it was the writer, Ivan Detbar, that walked off with the Emmy, right?

A trap the Crab was not about to walk into:

I'm not gonna go into that. Ivan's a good man.

So are you! Dig it everybody, the Crab Man!

That got applause. The Kid tapped his glass. But

neither was the Crab Man going to be a lickspittle for praise:

Bull pucky! You think everybody always loved the Crab? You think I was always on top? Overnight success? I'm here to tell you that that night took ten fucking years! Now you're making me mad!

Wild applause. Pleasely threw his arms up:

What did I do?

Keep it up, Pleasely.

Flushed and pleased, Pleasely implored the audience:

Hey, hey, don't egg him on!

The Crab delivered a thin-pitched bellyache of a whine:

I don't want an egg, I want my water!

After the laughter and applause, Pleasely downshifted:

Okay, okay, you grumpy crab. Now tell us about your costar, the luscious Little Miss Littlefield, tell us about her.

When the whistles and hoots died down, the Crab Man grumbled:

I won't tell you nothing.

Pleasely leaned closer:

You worked with her for six years. You must have something to tell.

Want me to tell you how on the set she don't wear underwear?

The audience went nuts.

Whoa! Really? How is it you happen to know this?

I happen to know this because I'm down there on the floor where you can see it! And let me tell you, Buster, Little Miss Littlefield is what you guys call a bottle blonde—the carpet don't match the drapes.

The audience cheered and jeered. The Crab Man took it further:

Remember that next time she's here pimping for the African Famine Relief.

Moans and groans. Pleasely shook his head:

My, my, do we sound a little bitter?

I lost an eye because of her.

The audience groaned again. Pleasely switched subjects:

So what do your friends call you?

I don't have none. If I did, they'd call me Pingo.

Why Pingo?

Cause I don't like Dingo!

Laughter. The rattle of claws. The Kid whispered the name, reached out, touched the screen, said it again:

Pingo.

The Crab Man seemed to sag and went reflective:

What's the difference? It's all fiddle and scuttle for a poor old crab, no big deal.

Hey, you've done pretty well for yourself, got a chauffeur, a tennis court with a pool, and a two-story mansion. Eh?

The Crab Man scoffed:

Don't confuse showbiz with real life, Buster. Yeah,

sure, I can swim, but I got no interest in tennis, and I live in a cell.

Like a prison?

No, like the Maharishi, or Swami Pravakananda. When I'm not working, I'm sitting in there like a monk contemplating my riddles.

Oh, really? Please, would you tell us one?

The Kid put down his drink and whispered:

Yeah, come on, tell one, Pingo!

The Crab Man took a moment to consider, then:

What is it takes longer to go down than it does to come up?

A submarine full of Russians?

That's not funny.

The tenth beer?

Forget it.

Come on, what's the answer?

If you're attacked by bees, don't jump in the lake.

What's that mean?

It means they'll be waiting for you when you come out.

I don't get it.

You will when I sic a hammerhead on your assplate, Buster!

The audience erupted. The Crab Man scuffled around on the box like he was going over the edge. Pleasely half rose.

Where you going?!

I gotta go clean my cell.

Hold on! What about your water?

You drink it!

The applause was wild. The Kid put down his drink, lifted his arms, snapping his fingers like pincers.

I t was a sunless noon. Mail-lady time. Abe appeared in the front window of his warehouse. He looked left, looked right, but the street was empty.

C arriers had their special spots to endure the swelter or the cold, places to kick back, a bathroom to use. Olympia had the Kid's, at least when his dad wasn't there.

The Kid was inquisitive, a scrutinizer, and she liked him for that. Also, they could be quiet together. Because Olympia was tall, he asked her if she was part Indian. She wasn't. The week before she asked him what he wanted to be when he grew up. He told her he would sell beer at the ballpark. They both knew it was a lie. He'd never been to the ballpark, didn't know where it was. She wagged a finger at him.

You just better behave yourself, Mister.

He loved being with her; besides being beautiful, she was funny. She thought he was too, but they never laughed.

They were sitting on the floor. He was helping her sort the day's mail, a job that needed concentration, but he had a question to ask.

Who's your favorite superhero?

Omar the Excluded.

Never heard of him.

He's sort of like Superman, except he can't fly.

She was putting the little piles of letters they'd stacked into her satchel.

So what's so super about him?

For one thing, he comes from a destroyed planet, so there's nothing he can't survive, but still, the other superguys won't team up with him.

Why not?

Because he's a drag.

She hoisted the bag over her shoulder. The Kid got to the door before she did and opened it. He watched her hang the bag on the trolley.

Is this Omar in the old zines?

Of course.

Could I get one?

If you got the money. They're not easy to get, they only put out a few.

What about the Crab Man, you like him?

Oh, please.

Abe Zinger, the guy across the street, he likes him. He's an artist.

He's an idiot.

He's a good painter.

That didn't make a difference to Olympia; she was on her way down the hall to the front door.

He wants to paint you!

She kept going, was almost at the exit.

That's what he said. He said that you're "sensational." And that's how he's gonna paint you.

The Kid couldn't tell if she hesitated or if it was just the way she went through the door. Then she was gone.

On a rainy day the year before, Olympia fell asleep on his couch for a minute and he watched her. It was the most intimate thing he'd even done with anyone, and it encouraged him to think that when he got old enough to get a driver's license, he and Olympia would probably get married.

He looked at himself in the bathroom mirror, finished gelling his thick black hair, then picked up a hand mirror and had a look at his profile. Impressed, he stepped back for a wider view. Addressing himself in Abe's voice and then his own:

What are you gonna do when you grow up? / I told you, interview the Crab Man.

Because of her day off, Olympia had some free time is what she told the Kid, and the Kid told Abe. Two days later it happened, a meeting was arranged. He rolled the cuffs of his jeans almost to his knees, then went to the kitchen, made himself a cup of instant coffee, drank it, then left for the warehouse.

A be figured that neither one of them knew enough about painting to know how good he was. How could they? But when he was done, they sure as hell would.

B y the way he stood at the easel, the Kid could tell Abe thought he was doing something important, but so far all he was doing was staring at Olympia.

She was wearing a short gray skirt, kneesocks, clunky brown shoes, her summer postal outfit, but it wasn't summer. The Kid could see goose bumps on her legs. He didn't like that Abe could see what he saw and didn't like that she cooperated so easily.

How do you want me?

Abe was so engrossed with what he was about to do, he didn't answer. A turtleneck is what he was wearing, paint-stained, pink, and too tight for a skinny guy, but it hid the blisters on his neck. The Kid sat on a stool, keeping a distance, but after a couple minutes of being ignored:

You guys know where Moscow is?

He wasn't expecting anybody to say Russia, but they didn't say anything.

In the barn, next to Pa's cow!

It was his favorite joke, but nobody laughed. Olympia

lifted her arms, dropped her head back. Abe kept staring at her but didn't lift his brush.

Then she tried another pose: got down on the floor, put her chin on her knees, pouting and pretty. Abe circled her, considering the angles, but didn't go back to his easel. The Kid hawked every move.

Olympia dragged a chair across the floor. Lounged on it, skirt hiked, legs splayed. Inspired, Abe finally began to paint. The Kid didn't say it too loud, but he said it:

Why don't you show him a little leg?

She acted like she didn't hear it. She was busy not moving. Abe was doing it in oil, sketching fiercely, his brush meticulous and quick, and his eyes never blinked. After a while, Olympia came to life on the canvas, and Abe seemed pleased. But Olympia was getting tired of posing, almost an hour had gone by.

When do I get to have a break?

Stay where you are!

She didn't seem surprised to be yelled at. The Kid was; it woke him up. Abe was almost done, but Olympia had begun to fidget. He tried to relax her.

So, what kind of mail the Kid get?

He doesn't—

Don't move!

He doesn't get any.

What about his dad, what's he get?

Postal workers aren't supposed to talk about other people's mail.

The Kid watched Abe smile and didn't like it. If it wasn't for him, Olympia wouldn't even be here. He could bring up the letter that Abe wrote, but wasn't sure how to go about it.

Does Abe get much mail?

For the first time, she looked at the Kid and was about to say something, but Abe didn't give her the chance.

The Kid says that you're hard to understand.

I never said that!

She didn't care who said what; Olympia was tired of being an artist's model.

Do I get any money for this?

The Kid was surprised to hear it brought up. Money was never mentioned. He waited to see what Abe would say, but Abe didn't say anything.

He's not gonna give you anything, are you, Abe?

Who said anything about money?

She did.

They were quiet awhile. Then the Kid had an idea.

Maybe he'll give you one of his paintings.

Abe acted like he didn't hear.

Look at that blimp, Olympia. Maybe you should take that.

Her eyes skimmed the walls, the jungle of colors, the brazen faces. She stopped on the blimp. Abe kept working, but he knew she was looking at it.

Put your head back like it was, please.

Olympia resumed her pose.

I'm not so sure I want that blimp, if that's what it is.

Abe stopped painting.

What did you say?

I'm not so sure that I like it, the blimp.

The Kid was disappointed to hear it and came to the blimp's defense.

When you like a blimp, you like it all the way, doesn't make any difference if you're not sure. Right, Abe?

That's right, Kid.

The Kid got to his feet; he was feeling better now.

Maybe you'd like it more if there was a dog in it.

Abe never heard anything so stupid.

No dogs!

Sniffing the nozzles.

There's no nozzles!

There's gotta be, else how could it get inflated?

It's already inflated!

The Kid didn't care, he stuck with the dog.

What about a Chihuahua, Olympia?

Olympia was starting to like the idea.

A Chihuahua? Bet a Chihuahua would be hard to paint. It's hard to say: A *Chihuahua would* . . .

Not for the Kid it wasn't:

A chihuahuawouldachihuahuawould.

He did it without a hitch, but the painting Abe just finished was what got the attention. Abe lifted it off the easel and held it up to show. Olympia's beauty looked uprooted, scrambled, urgent but easy, almost floating.

The grace of flesh and bone, the bushy butter of her hair, the luster of her skin, and the dark of her eyes, all of it simple, but grave, unforced. The Kid didn't like it, didn't like Abe showing off.

Take the blimp, Olympia. The blimp is better, don't you think?

But the blimp was forgotten; her heart was touched by poor, scrawny, hardworking Abe. Fact was, the painting captivated her.

How did you do it so fast? It's really good! You gotta sign it!

Why, thank you, Olympia. It's just a preliminary sketch, really.

It could be worth lots of money. It should be in a museum.

The Kid laughed—it sounded like a bark. Abe looked right at him.

You oughta get an appointment with Doctor Zitmore, Kid.

Who?

Abe tapped the corner of his mouth. The Kid had a pimple there. There was a sudden quiet. Olympia came closer, reached out to touch it—now she was having a go at him. The Kid batted her hand away, and it was Abe's turn to laugh:

See Zitmore, Kid.

He looked from Abe to Olympia, hated the way she was smiling at him.

It's right to have a pimple at a certain age. Who knows, you might have to start shaving someday.

Listen to her, Kid, words of wisdom.

The Kid knew it wasn't wisdom, it was bullshit, and he wanted to go. But he couldn't move. Affliction was in play, and Abe realized it, that it was unseemly to have picked on a ten-year-old. Abe decided to rectify it:

Hey, nobody's at fault here. We're all part of the same event. I couldn't have done this without you guys, but sometimes things get wobbly, we don't know what and don't know why. It's like a Johnny thing.

Johnny who?

The Kid could have told her, but he's not up for it yet. Abe takes it:

It's an Insteadman kind of thing, or a Howeverman kind of thing. A bowl of pet chow and the sound of the dog in the yellow pavilion of the owner's ear. American men with nutmeg on their shorts, the heels of their wives' mules encrusted with droppings of one kind or another. A one-armed guy in the moonlight pissing in the grass, smoking a cigarette kind of thing.

What are you talking about?

Abe could tell she wasn't comfortable with unusual ideas, so he tried to explain:

First person singular talking to himself in third. Johnny plays the field. Right, Kid? Normal-minded folks enclosed by what goes on in the corners of their eyes. Like a painting. Life in the streets. *The Crab's Welcome.*

The Kid was glad that Abe brought the Crab into it and nodded emphatically. Olympia didn't want to hear about the Crab Man, but she was curious about the streets:

What streets?

Brooklyn streets.

The Kid corrected him:

Red Hook.

Same difference. Then back to the keyholes up on the Upper East Side. Now I hear he's out west.

Maybe so, but this is still Red Hook, Abe.

Abe didn't care, he'd gone beyond that:

We have to look forward now. It's your call, Kid. Your future. And your tall friend here, if she wants to come, she can.

And the three of them departed, left the slanted light of the warehouse for a darker place. A windowless room with one door. In the center of the room, a man-size cage with straw on the floor. That's where the Crab Man squats.

The door of the room was partly open. A piece of the street could be seen, quiet and bright out there. He lived without perks, but got no credit for it. People rarely came around, but he left the door open anyway so air could get in, evaporate the fumes.

When he heard the whispering behind him he held his breath, too proud to turn. Besides his missing eye, now a claw was gone, and he didn't feel like swiveling. Either it was hooligans or fans, he couldn't tell.

Present yourselves, intruders!

Olympia, Abe, and the Kid came around to the front of the pen to face the Crab Man. Skeptical of straw encrusted with who-knew-what, Abe backed up a step. This was the Kid's call.

The Crab Man didn't care for tall people, especially women. But Abe was short and that was good. The Kid even shorter, a good size for the Crab, and since the cell was elevated a couple feet off the floor, it was almost an eye-to-eye proposition.

What are you looking at?

The Kid couldn't say, but he didn't look away.

State your business!

The Kid had questions, but being face-to-face with the actual Crab Man took his breath away. It was up to Abe.

The Kid wants to talk to you, Crab Man. Plus the door was open.

So is the Strait of Hormuz, but that doesn't mean you gotta go sailing through it.

That was a laugh line, but nobody laughed. The Crab was dealing with duds. Suddenly, the Kid sat down on the floor. A good move. It made the Crab Man feel taller and relaxed the vibe a little. But Olympia wasn't comfortable. There was a sting of chlorine in the air and it burned her nose. She spotted a model airplane on the floor by the door and knew there was no way the Crab could ever fly it, not even if he had his other claw.

What happened to your claw?

An impertinent question, which he ignored—didn't even look at her—from somebody he didn't like in the first place.

Water was dripping somewhere. The Crab Man made a scratching sound. He was smaller than the Kid had imagined and not so rambunctious as he was on TV, plus his shell looked bleached. The Crab no longer owned the purpose and push of his younger days. He was getting on. His voice was tinny and thin, but still severe:

You guys got any money?

The trio looked blank. For sure the Kid didn't. Abe had five bucks, but he wasn't about to give it to the Crab Man. Olympia had more than Abe, but she was being ignored.

Pikers and deadbeats! How am I supposed to support myself? You may as well eat me!

Another laugh line, but still no laughs. Abe didn't know what else to say, so he said it again:

The Kid wants to interview you.

I don't do interviews.

Suddenly the Kid spoke up, loud too.

You do too, I saw you!

Saw me where?

Last night on *Buster Pleasely*.

That was a rerun, stupid.

That stunned everybody, even the Crab—he didn't mean to be so mean. Too late. For sure it was a bad moment for the Kid. And to make it worse, Olympia came to his rescue.

The Kid pays close attention to you, you and your career. He's your biggest fan, and he was hoping for you to cooperate on this.

No, I wasn't!

Olympia didn't pay any attention. The Crab pissed her off:

What difference does it make if it was a rerun? He still saw it, and it made him curious.

No, it didn't!

He wants to know about you.

No, I don't!

Yes, he does. You see what you've done?

Like an arrow, she said it right in the Crab's face:

He stuck his neck out coming here!

The Crab Man didn't have a neck, but he got the idea. Now that he had a closer look at her, he understood how they got his address. He was impressed by uniforms, insignias, and the like, especially postal outfits.

I'll tell him anything he wants to know. What do you wanna know, Kid?

This was the way the Kid dreamed it, but not with

Abe and Olympia there. They were all waiting to hear what he was about to say, and he was about to, but Olympia butted in again:

He wants to know who . . . or what your father was.

Postal uniform or not, the Crab wasn't going to let her get personal:

You got all the answers, doll, you tell me.

She didn't back up an inch:

Your father was a tiler.

The Kid thought he knew everything about the Crab Man, but he didn't know that. Abe too, he'd never heard such a thing, and asked:

What do you mean, a tiler?

Without taking her eyes off the Crab, Olympia told Abe the answer.

As in tiles. A roof tiler. That's how come he had a fear of heights. He took a fall and never recovered. Isn't that right?

The Crab Man blows a bubble:

No, that's not right. That was just publicity. Take no stock in the tabloids, my dear. It was TB that killed my father. Some call it crab-lung. He was from Tierra del Fuego; it's cold down there, but my lungs are fine.

The Kid got to his feet. It was now or never:

Vomiting sailors in a submarine isn't it. I know that.

He didn't have the facial muscles to show it, but the Crab Man was perplexed by this.

Excuse me? Isn't what?

What goes down faster than it comes up. The answer to your riddle.

It's the other way around, Kid—what comes up faster than it goes down. But you're blunt, I'll give you that.

The Kid was thrilled to hear it, but smart enough not to show it. Encouraged, he offered another option:

It's not a rocket either.

And it never will be. Blunt, but dumber than a fart. Just joking. I know you're smart. If I was still doing the show, I'd write you a part. Him too.

Abe was happy to be included.

I'm a painter.

I could tell by your shoes. I'd give you a brush and a pail, have you work on the sets.

He had excluded Olympia on purpose so he could better highlight the answer to the question that she previously asked.

Lost the claw in an accident, doll. My chauffeur was having trouble, I tried to help, and he slammed the door on it.

She winced at the thought of it, and the Crab Man softened:

Of course, time takes its toll, Olympia. We crabs sometimes lose our appendages, too much snip-snip. Who knows, though, it could grow back, you know what I mean?

She did know, he could see it in her eyes. He was beginning to feel fond of her and the Kid most of all:

My mother's name was Sally. There's a picture of her over there if any of you care to have a look.

The three of them drifted over to a framed eight-by-ten of a heavyset woman wearing overalls under a muddy skirt under a rain slicker posing against a rock with a crash of wave spray behind her.

Now Abe needed a bathroom, but the only door in the room was to the street. The Crab Man had no need of a bathroom. Piss and shit didn't bother him. Only about three things did: fire, hammers, and snow. Of course there was lightning and certain sorts of birds that distressed him, especially seagulls. He despised their screams and was glad he didn't live by the sea. But generally, the Crab had the shape and discipline to withstand the forces of Nature and was feeling pretty good about himself at the moment. Chummy, in fact.

The Kid here is small, like me; fortunately, that's probably gonna change. If he doesn't die first.

Abe was shocked:

Die? What are you talking about?

Excuse me, Abe, I was not finished. You capitalize on such an idea I just said—this dying business, as opposed to putting your head in the sand.

But still, people live longer than crabs, don't they? Especially a young person. Why would he die first?

Abe was starting to get on the Crab Man's nerves:

Because sooner or later, that's what we do, Abe. Have you never noticed?

The Kid had:

Could I quote you on that, Pingo?

No one ever called him that before.

Of course you can! Come over here, Kid.

Olympia backed away for the privacy of it. Abe too. The Kid stooped down, got his face between the bars, and turned his head, giving the Crab his ear. The Crab Man strained forward and whispered something. The Kid laughed, then straightened up. The Crab Man was excited, his one eye gleaming.

If I had arms, I'd give this little sucker a hug!

O n their way back to Red Hook, Abe wanted to know what the Crab Man had whispered. Was it the answer to the riddle? The Kid said nothing.

Olympia told him to mind his own business. Abe figured it *was* his business; he was interested in the Crab Man's thoughts, the vicissitudes of the spirit, the twists and turns of mortality. But the Kid stayed quiet. It would have to wait.

That night after his contemplations, the Crab Man had a good sleep with a dream in it. It was a sleep from which he would never wake. But before that happened, he dreamt he was in the aisle of a well-lit supermarket and the Kid took him for a fast ride in a shopping cart.

THE
CLIMACTERIC
OF ZACKARY
RAY

Before there was a Kevin Spacey, there was John Malkovich. Before there was a John Malkovich, there was Zackary Ray. He was taller and more elegant than his successors, but he lacked their range. He was from an older school of acting. No school. He graduated Cornell with a B.A. in business and went to Madison Avenue. At Barnbach Yardhouse & Young, the art department is where he wanted to be, but marketing is what he got. After a year of Maytag and the Jolly Green Giant, he got systolic hypertension, inflammation of the inner ear, and dizzy spells.

It may have been a protracted case of psittacosis he caught from playing with his roommate's macaw. That's what the doctor thought, but Zackary knew better: It was the stress from his job. He quit and found a new place to live. In the time it took to recover, he reconsidered his career and went back to his first love, the theater. He would give it a try, and if it didn't happen he would move on. But it did happen. He was cast in an off-Broadway spoof that led to a Broadway hit that ran seven months. Hollywood took notice, and Zackary was the only actor in the play invited west for the film version.

A year later he married the producer's daughter and tried to be a family man, but that's not who he played. He was the best of his generation at catfooted lassitude bordering on the malefic. Best at being obsessed by the impossibility of a lady's favor. Famous for playing conniving characters, half craven, half courageous, and never showing their hands. *The gears of corruption lubricated with honey,* as one reviewer put it. The critics loved him and the audiences loved to hate him. He sided with Nazis, made deals with Japs. Ruthless in slippers and brocaded gown, he could whisper something in a lady's ear, then shoot her with a sigh.

He was Baltimore born-and-bred, but there was something Old World about him, lean and unholy with his icy blue eyes, but he only played Americans, except for once. In the late fifties he was cast as Judas Iscariot in a star-studded biblical epic. For a touch of sympathy he decided to give Judas a limp, but the director nixed it. The only thing Zackary liked about that role was the cloak. And the money. To save some, the studio cheated Utah for Jerusalem and shot in early spring to avoid the heat—but snow was what they got, and it didn't stop. Millions were wasted on waiting, and Zackary made a bundle doing nothing till July.

He already owned a house in Brentwood, but had to buy another in Malibu, for his wife. No divorce, just separate houses. Their son grew up in both. Then the son was gone, Zackary didn't know where; even if he did, he knew it wouldn't help. He felt guilty about this and guiltier still that he didn't feel more guilty. As a father and husband, he hadn't amounted to much.

His career expanded then diminished. A slump is what he called it, and it spread. For about twelve years running, he was among the best of the bad guys, but then they had seen enough. For the next twelve, except for a couple DUIs, he couldn't get arrested.

A life sentence without possibility of surprise. It was boring in Brentwood. Being a specialist at portraying malignity could have an effect on a person. He was a disciplined and reliable actor, but nothing felt authentic anymore. Twelve years was a long time to be washed up.

Sometimes, alone at night and having gone too far with the gin, he wrote letters to his agent. Not his true agent—his true agent was dead. That was Leonard; this was Sid, the son. He'd taken over the agency, and kept Zackary around because it was easier than dropping him. He was twenty-four years old and wore tennis shoes to the office. Zack would write single-spaced, five-page indictments blaming everything from the war in Southeast Asia to his answering service for the slump. Then, trying to be upbeat, would remind Sid that he still got fan mail requesting autographs and eight-by-tens, that he was relevant still and could be brought to the money. Sid didn't have the stamina to read this shit, but for a laugh, sometimes he passed these letters around to his friends.

Zackary kept a bottle in his Buick and a silver flask in the inside pocket of his coat. Gin. A tough guy's drink, and a lady's too. At its best, life was tenuous. No wonder people believed in miracles—but not him, he would take it standing up.

The linen suit. It might be too much. Too much what? He wasn't sure. But he was on the road before noon. Indio. Not even Palm Springs. *The National Radio Advertisers and Broadcasters of America and International Affiliates from the English-Speaking World* is what the flier said. No invitation. But he had done some radio work in his day, they knew who he was—he wouldn't be turned away.

Lorenzo and his wife, Belle, would probably be there. He tried to recall if he had worn the same suit the last time he saw her. The parking lot, Belle in his arms. It happened before, it could happen again. Zackary stopped for a date shake just outside of Indio. Drank half of it in the car. His stomach wasn't good.

CELEBRATING 55 YEARS OF BROADCASTING, the banner read. It was an airless evening, around ninety degrees, and no place to park near the entrance. Inside, the air-conditioning made his sweat feel like ice. At the buffet he swayed a little, having a bit of a hard time keeping his balance. But just the right kind of hard time. If any of the old flacks recognized him and approached, he would just chew his gum and nod his head, let them think what they thought and move on.

Lorenzo had done well. Standing between tables, they had a conversation, the three of them. Lorenzo was there to give a speech on how to circumvent pitfalls on the road to success, and didn't ask Zackary a single question. And Zackary only got to ask Belle one. What was she up to these days? Lorenzo answered it.

Belle had gone back to school, going to be an insurance adjuster, big money there. Age had softened her, but not much. If anything it made her more beautiful. Zackary wanted to tell her she looked like Cleopatra. But Lorenzo couldn't stop talking about himself. Poor asshole, even in his elevator shoes he only came up to her chin. If Zackary was patient maybe he could get her alone, something could happen. It had before.

Go out there and wait in the parking lot, see if she comes. But she never even really looked at him. Hello, you're looking fit, and that was about it. Not even that. Lorenzo didn't leave any room for it. Maybe Belle had told him what had happened in the parking lot at Chasen's three years earlier, or was it four? This was a different parking lot, but after a visit to the men's room, that's where Zackary went.

And suddenly there she was. Fifteen feet away, had just come out the back door. She saw him, didn't move. He came closer.

So how's life, Belle?

I'm not happy with it, Zack. Not even close.

What are you going to do?

He meant it to be a wide-ranging, all-purpose sort of question, but she was specific.

I came out to have a smoke.

She could have smoked inside. Was she being coy? He came closer to light it. She lit it herself.

You have a funny way of putting things, he said.

What do you want?

Nothing. Been a while since we talked.

What's to talk about?

Maybe she was drunk. He was fine, a little nervous, but fine. There were lots of things to talk about.

Any number of things. You, me . . .

Back off.

He wasn't close enough to back off, but he did. She flipped her cigarette.

I'm going back inside.

He liked a little touch-and-go, a bit of mystery, but not this much. He had just wanted to look into her eyes and see her look back like he was something special. When she went through the door, he could hear applause.

H e waited in his car, listening to the radio, watching those who hadn't already driven away drive away. The prospect of going back to Brentwood right then made him empty. What was to go back to? Some he guessed would stay, spend the night in palmy motels, but Zackary was worried about money and ended up at a place called the Bottom Dollar that didn't have a pool. He woke up at sunrise but stayed in bed till noon.

He drove south through Penstock and Yuings, gaunt little towns with nothing in between, down to Guyacola, a place he had been once before. It was even less than it was the last time he saw it. He parked in front of a bar called the Snake Pit. It was closed, had the dusty look of a place that had been that way awhile. No people, no traffic, except for a pickup parked down the street with a sheepdog sleeping on the roof.

He turned off the engine, lowered the window. It was hot, but he traded the AC for the silence. Overhead the sky was still and blue, but twenty miles to the west a cluster of black clouds hung over the mountains. He could see lightning out there and listened for thunder, but it was too far away.

It was from those mountains, down from a place called Fulgar, that he had come the last time, which was the first time he stopped in Guyacola. Because of a bottle.

A jug really, a half gallon of apple juice that he never opened. Kept it on the shelf above his bed. The label was what he liked. A golden sun over a grove of palms in the luminous style of Maxfield Parrish. He had never taken a close look at the fine print below the illustration. Then one night he did.

He looked up Fulgar in *The Thomas Guide*. Found it in lowercase on a row of mountains somewhere between the ocean and the desert, wasn't even a town. He had an impulse to go, but didn't, didn't have the get-up-and-go for a lark at that point. He waited till fall. On the fourteenth of October, his birthday, he got in the Buick and went. Drove down the coast sixty miles, then east for almost an hour up into the mountains and found the place. APPLE CAPITAL OF THE WORLD, a sign said. But he didn't see any apple trees. Fulgar was basically a gas station plus the Happy Apple, which was a combination country store–café with four stools and a counter.

He ordered the specialty and a cup of coffee. "Known far and wide for our stuffed *you-know-what* baked in brown sugar, cinnamon, raisins and walnuts melted in country butter" is what the menu said. Zack had one and ordered another to go. No matter how much he ate, he never gained weight. He had the metabolism of a ferret and fucked like one, his wife once said.

That was as close to a compliment as she ever came. He asked the old lady who served him where the desert was. The road he came up on seemed to have ended, but there was another that went down the eastern face of the mountain, and she told him how to get to it and to be careful because it was steep and twisty. It was too; it felt like driving down the side of the moon, and when he got to the bottom the desert was there, went all the way to the great Salton Sea, which he had never seen, but since it was there he drove in that direction to have a look.

Traveling fast and flat through a world of red ants and rattlesnakes excited him, and he was glad he came. There were dunes and silence, no population of people to see, just an occasional car whizzing by. The landscape beguiled and he wanted to walk in it, take off his shoes and socks, feel the sand on his feet. He did park and walk, but not too far from the car. He loved the desert, but didn't trust it and kept his shoes on.

Through and around mesquite and other thorny things, he walked over the gravelly sand to the dune he came to climb, but changed his mind when he got to the base of it. It was a bad idea to blotch it with footprints; also he didn't want to get sand in his shoes.

He heard the gibbering of something he couldn't see. He scanned the sky, the ground. Probably a roadrunner. He spotted a rusted beer can. Some stupid bastard drank it then left it, crushed it too. Zackary could bury it, but what good would it do, where would it end? The lunatic prophets wandering the deserts in bygone days probably left their crap as well. Zackary unscrewed his flask and drank to the extinction of louts and their products, then hollered as loud as he could:

The reptiles will not be conquered!

He had done to the silence what he didn't want to do

to the dune, and looked around to make sure he was alone. Nothing was deserted in the desert; the only thing that didn't belong was him, yet his presence complicated nothing. He looked over his shoulder to make sure the Buick was still there. Nothing had moved.

Then something did. A turtle the size of a soup bowl was going somewhere. Zackary slipped the flask back into his pocket and went closer. The turtle stopped. Neither of them moved. Zackary yelled at it. The turtle stayed put. Zackary flapped his arms. The turtle withdrew into its shell. He nudged it with his foot. The turtle stayed shut. He bent down for a closer look.

At toy stores, Zackary bought Rubik's Cubes to fiddle with. He was good at geometry, liked fractional color-coded shapes (he was of Swiss lineage; he liked Paul Klee). The turtle's shell was oval, but within it there were octagons, hexagons, and nonagons. The welded masonry of its back was moth brown with glimmers of green. He could take this turtle home, put it in the yard, bring in sand, a rock garden maybe, plant cactus. He could call the turtle Euclid.

A jug of apple juice he never drank triggered a trip he had no reason to take and he winds up with a turtle. Anything could happen, things added up. Carefully, he lifted it off the ground, holding it away from himself—a turtle didn't have many options, but it could piss on you. Zackary set it back down. On its back. Capsized, immediately its head and legs appeared, wagging, thrashing for solid ground. He watched it struggle a moment, then

HAMPTON FANCHER

flipped it over, right side down. In no hurry, the turtle waddled away. It wasn't going to Brentwood.

Zackary was hungry, his back hurt, and he wanted a shower. On the road he had passed a sign that said GUYACOLA 5 MILES.

The Firefly Motel had a thirty-foot pole with a light on top that blinked and seven one-room cabins. Zackary took number seven. He took a shower, a shot of gin, and went back out before the sun went down.

There was the hardware store, a Mexican market, and the China Diner. None of it looked inviting. The Snake Pit was open. That's where he went.

It was a big hollow place with a concrete floor and stucco walls. Four locals, five including the barman, huddled at one end of the bar. Three of them were young; the fourth was larger, shorter, and older, pushing fifty. He was doing the talking, but stopped when Zackary walked in.

Borrego Bill was big-chested, slit-eyed, and neckless, shoe-polish black hair, pants, boots, and shirt all black, a turquoise ring on his pinky. Zackary had seen the type before; on the sets of Westerns, extras like him were not unusual.

The bar was long, and Zackary took a seat at the lonesome end. And waited. They acted like he wasn't there.

What did he expect, applause? He'd been around, knew the routine; there was rule of rank in a place like this. Borrego had names for his guys that proved it;

called the big one Bonehead, the smallest Peewee, and the one in between Ratbreath. After another minute, Borrego told the barman, whose name was Bob, to attend to the customer.

Zackary ordered a draft please. No draft, just bottles. On the wall next to the American Legion plaque was a Schlitz ad. He ordered one. Bob brought it without a glass. It was warm.

It felt like *Bad Day at Black Rock*. Spencer Tracy played a one-armed stranger comes into a two-bit town, and right off he's harassed by louts. Tracy looks way too old to win a fight and won't engage, but neither does he back down. He's insulted, run off the road, threatened, and goaded until he's had enough. Then his tormentors find out what an older man with one arm can do if he studied martial arts in Japan.

Zackary loved that movie. Who didn't? Always he wanted to play a part like that, the one who wins at the end. But they would never let him. Now he couldn't get hired to play one of the bad guys the hero beats up.

Right then a man came into the Snake Pit who never won anything. Reed Fingley was small, twitchy, and needed inclusion. He muttered a salutation not expecting a response and didn't get one, then took a stool close as he could to the others.

Borrego resumed his monologue. Zackary tried to hear what he was saying, but the acoustics were boomy. The bullfrog talked and the tadpoles listened. Zackary sipped his Schlitz. Life was full of traps, self-made and otherwise; he wanted out, but to leave right then would have endorsed their victory. He would finish his beer first. Although he declined to look, Zackary knew Borrego's performance was meant for him.

He brought out his phone book, pretended to search for a number. Already in the G's before he realized Reed Fingley was standing two feet away talking to him. Timid, apologetic, but eager, explaining something about time management. Zackary pocketed his phone book and listened. Reed had been teaching at Yucaipa Community College, until he was forced to retire because of his health. Then he talked about his dog, Royal Gallant. Often racehorses have two names, why not dogs? Zackary agreed, then asked him what breed of dog it was. Reed wasn't sure, but thought he might have had some Lab in him. Did have. Royal Gallant recently died. Reed had just buried him in the front yard of his trailer. No flowers, no stone, just buried, he said. Then changed the subject, went back to time.

There's four thousand ways to classify it. My specialty was histograms.

Zack was out of his depth, but not completely.

Overlapping or cumulative?

You mean consecutive or disjointed.

Tell me, I'm here to learn.

Okay then! The quantifying of comparabilities to the disparities of the temporarily contiguous is what that is.

That sounds like a contradiction with real opportunities.

Reed was excited to hear it, to be talking to someone who understood, a professional man. And intrigued by Reed's train of thought, even though he couldn't quite catch it, Zackary was glad to have somebody to talk to in the Snake Pit.

Borrego and the boys weren't glad at all, didn't like their little egghead getting all chummy with Mr. Good Listener from somewhere else. Borrego hung his head, and Peewee made vomiting sounds.

Either Reed didn't notice or didn't care; he kept talking.

One interval split into two that looks like a union equivalence may or may not have a fracture value, because if one is nullified, the other is transferred. You understand?

Sounds like marriage, Zackary said.

The stranger was not only smart, he was funny. Encouraged, Reed went on.

You see, the transfer function is going to be identical to the second one no matter what the first one is.

What's the second one?

The assumption that they're going to be the same.

But they aren't?

Nope, Euclidean-based distances can't be reduced by volume unless you do it by midpoint intervals. Which leads to what?

Give me a hint.

One varies, the other is constant, but if they're doing it together, they're neither.

What's that called?

Diffusion puzzle. I wrote the manual on it. You come over, I'll give you one.

Reed put out his hand and they shook on it, exchanged names. The El Dorado trailer park is where he lived, number four. Reed wrote it down on a napkin, then squinted around to see who was looking. They were all looking. The barman cleared his throat. Borrego moaned. Zackary smiled at him. Borrego turned away. Ratbreath yelled:

Get out of here, Reed!

Number four, Reed whispered, there's a lemon tree next to the door. I'll give you a manual, make you a martini!

The way he skimmed across the floor and out the door reminded Zackary of Groucho Marx.

The only sound left was the swamp cooler. Zackary would have liked another beer, but the Snake Pit felt concluded. And there was gin in the car. He laid a five dollar bill on the bar and left.

One place to eat. The China Diner. There was nothing Chinese on the menu. The Chinese had left town. The new owner and his wife hadn't come up with a name yet. That's what the waitress told him. And she didn't think they ever would.

The memory of her gave him a pang. She couldn't have been more than twenty. She was innocent and fun, she was pretty. Probably still pretty and has three kids by now. Zackary tried, but couldn't remember her name. The air was clear still, but a little darker; the sun had gone down. Those clouds over the mountains had thickened, were coming closer.

The war in Vietnam had gotten a foothold, young men in small towns had signed up and gone. The only thing young in the place was the waitress. A broad innocent smile, peachy lips, and beautiful teeth. She was an orchid in a vacant lot. A couple of elders at the counter, but the booths were empty. Zackary took one in the back. Had the waitress to himself. She watched him study the menu. The wrinkled linen suit, his aquamarine eyes, he even had a book. She was dazzled and didn't try to hide it. Did he want the special? Chicken cacciatore. He wanted breakfast. It was almost closing time. Could she make it happen?

When she brought him scrambled eggs and toast he was reading. She cocked her head to peek at the title. He held the book up so she could see it. The cover was a photo of a naked foot propped on a steamer trunk in front of a window overlooking the sea. She pronounced the title in a whisper: *Death in Venice*. He gave her an encouraging nod and she asked him if he believed in reincarnation.

He didn't believe in much of anything, he said, except that life always seemed to be changing addresses. She wasn't sure what that meant, but loved how he said it. So did he. Life is like a curve, he told her, and what is it that curves don't have? She didn't know. Points, he said. Her smile widened. He could see her molars.

The conjectures of transcendence, people who be-lieved in voodoo and prayer, holy scriptures, the con-junctions of planets, made him uneasy, but with her it was a charm. The warmth of his attention and the self-mockery of his pronouncements excited her—she was flattered and flushed, and he was excited back at her.

Before coming in, Zackary had drunk of his flask. His powers had grown large around her. He invited her to sit. She explained that even if it were allowed, she couldn't; she had a boyfriend and people would talk. Where was this boyfriend? In Vietnam, fighting the war. She called him Arvid Toby. Two first names: Zack-ary wondered if Arvid Toby knew Royal Gallant.

She met Arvid Toby in high school, but they didn't date till just before he left. And what did she think of the war? Not much, because she didn't know what it was about. Zackary told her that nobody did, that's why it was a bad idea. She agreed. She didn't know Zackary was in the movies either. She didn't know who Thomas Mann was. She didn't know where Vietnam was. Zackary knew that in a woman who had nothing to hide, the best was hidden.

He could wait in the parking lot till after the diner closed, and if she decided to and the coast was clear, they could continue to discuss all the wonderful things she didn't know, out there. She wouldn't promise she would, but didn't say she wouldn't. He would just have to wait and see.

He sat in the Buick and waited. The last time he had

sex in a car it was in a Lincoln Continental. He liked the word *classy*; never said it, but he thought it and felt that he had it. A kind of dusty élan that made him feel deserving of something better than he usually got. Sometimes he got it. He appealed to Rita. She fucked him one night in the back of that Lincoln Continental. He couldn't remember whose. She was drunk. He wasn't; it happened before he got the chance. It still bothered him she may have done it on a bet. He had no good reason to think it, but he did. He heard it somewhere, that she had sex with somebody on a bet, and he was afraid it may have been him. Rita wasn't too bright, but there was something touching about her. Plus she was Rita fucking Hayworth. Cansino was her real last name, a Chicana from East L.A.

He only saw her twice. That once in the Lincoln and the next time, which was the last time, in Rome. He had been out with a group of Swedes and wound up at Giorgio de Chirico's apartment at the bottom of the Spanish Steps. He and the old painter sat on a couch discussing Mussolini, bananas, and trains. The gin flowed, and de Chirico showed Zackary a sketch he had done of an Eskimo holding a rope tied to the neck of a giraffe standing in front of what looked to be the Great Pyramid of Giza. Zackary loved it and hoped the old man might give it to him. But at sunup he left with hugs and handshakes, but without the sketch, and climbed the Spanish Steps to the Hotel Excelsior.

Instead of the lobby, he went in a side door, through the lounge where jazz was nightly played. It was dark and empty except for two drunks asleep at the bar. It was Rita and her boyfriend, Gary Merrill, a decent guy and not a bad actor. Probably she was in Rome to work, like Zackary was. Gary might have been along for the ride, or the other way around. This was the early sixties, lots of Hollywood people in town for Italian movie work. He felt bad for both of them.

Now he felt bad for himself. The waitress hadn't shown up. There was nothing worth listening to on the radio, and the flask was empty. He was about to drive away when a Toyota pickup went by, turned the corner, and parked. It was her. His was the only car in the lot; looking this way and that, she hurried right to it. He opened the passenger door and she slid in. She had changed her shoes, put on fresh lipstick, but no time for a shower. She smelled like Clorets and fried chicken.

He told her how glad he was that she came. Told her how good she looked, but she was so nervous she could hardly look at him. The magnetic reciprocity they'd shared in the diner was gone. He offered her a cigarette. She didn't smoke. If he hadn't finished off the flask, he could have given her gin. Clark Gable might work, she would know who that was. A decade earlier he'd been invited to the King's fiftieth-birthday party. An event worth telling. Zackary slipped the cigarette back in the pack and was about to get started when suddenly she said she should go. But she didn't move. It was up to him. Gentleman Zack got out of the car, went around to her side, and opened the door. He gave her his hand and she rose.

They stood full-length against each other, using the car as a backstop, his long strong fingers laced around her narrow waist. He kissed her throat, her face, her hair. She only stopped him a little from doing more, but he did and she let him. He slid down her body to his knees. She clutched his head to her belly. Under her sweater, his face smashed against her flesh made it hard to breathe, but he didn't care.

Suddenly she convulsed and made a sound that sounded like he hurt her. He looked up. One of her hands covering her mouth, looking straight ahead, she moaned, Oh, no.

He should have known. Three from the Snake Pit, Ratbreath, Peewee, and Bonehead, coming across the lot. Arvid Toby's girl caught in flagrante on the verge of delicto. The least Zackary could expect was a battering and not lose any teeth. Where was Borrego? Probably waiting around the corner with a hammer.

Stranger inflicts indecencies on resident sweetheart cried out for punishment. He was due for some damnation, but not on his knees. As he rose, one of them made a threat he didn't quite catch. Zackary thought of a line from a film he no longer remembered the title of. Didn't yell it, delivered it in a stage whisper:

Come a little closer, boys, I'll let you get to know me.

They'd never heard anything so screwy. The perversity of it crimped their momentum. Peewee yelled:

He was kissing her down there!

You stupid bastards, he wasn't either!

The snarl of her defiance impressed everyone. Then a burst of insults and warnings were exchanged. Rat-breath had a can of beer he threatened to throw. She gave him the finger. He threw it. She dodged the can and showed them a moment of disdain before walking as fast as she could without actually running back to her Toyota.

Then it was the rooster show. Bonehead coming closer, almost dancing. Zackary standing his ground, letting them know he would do them some damage before he went down. But just as it was about to happen, coming across the lot, voice like a Klaxon, Borrego was there.

What are you dickweeds doing?

Savoring the importance of his own arrival, he waited for a response. They all stepped on one another trying to tell him what just happened. Borrego knew what had happened, he'd been watching, told them get back to the Snake Pit or go home to bed. He would handle things now.

He was trying to fuck her, Bill!

Borrego wasn't going to say it again. Beat the shit out of this guy then run back to the Snake Pit and tell

Borrego is what they wanted to do, and now here was Borrego telling them not to. They didn't know what to do. They evil-eyed Zackary, and one of them grumbled, another one spit, then they obeyed.

Zackary and Borrego watched the three slink off across the street, then without looking at him, Borrego said:

Got any complaints about the Firefly?

Zackary wasn't sure what he was talking about.

You mean the motel?

If you do, I'd be the one to tell.

Zack stared at him—why would he be the one to tell?

I own it.

Borrego was puffed up and sly; was he waiting for a compliment? Zackary decided to be careful.

I thought fireflies were an eastern insect, didn't know you had 'em out here.

Yeah, we got 'em. Firefly ain't really even a fly. What they are is soft-bodied beetles that light up when they get horny.

Zackary wasn't sure if things were getting better or they just got worse. Borrego was looking right at him.

You probably think I'm coldhearted, right?

Why would I think that?

I mean back at the bar. I was watching you. A guy in your position is used to people trying to get something off him. You gotta protect yourself, I understand that.

He came closer.

Those boys aren't old enough to know who you are, or else they'd be running home saying, "Guess who I saw?!" Be asking for your autograph. I'm Bill.

He clapped his hands a couple times and grinned.

What do you say we go over and have a drink?

It wasn't a good time to say no. Back to the Snake Pit, Borrego telling him the score.

A man like yourself can't be expected to know how things work in a place like this. This ain't Beverly Hills. Gonna hit on somebody else's girl, you best not be doing it in the parking lot. You'd have done better sneaking it back into the Firefly.

Zackary followed him into the Snake Pit. Except for Bob and the boys, the place was still empty. Borrego guided Zackary to a table.

Bob brought over a bottle of whiskey and two glasses. Borrego poured one for his guest and one for himself.

Whiskey's okay?

Yeah, it's fine.

Here's to little Reed Fingley.

Clink and down the hatch. Borrego poured again.

Discouraged, Bonehead, Peewee, and Ratbreath watched from the bar. Zackary gave a glance. They looked away. Borrego snorted.

They wanted to kick your ass.

They should join the army.

You're right. The little one wants to, wants to go in the Marines. The other one there, he tried, but they're not gonna take him. And the big one, he's got something wrong with his feet. But things get bad enough, who knows, they could take him.

Zackary relaxed a bit, not because of the whiskey— he didn't like it—but because show-dog dipsos were familiar territory, and Borrego was definitely that.

You know how long Fingley's been waiting for somebody who could understand what the hell he's talking about? You see how glad he was?

Reed?

Yep, you made him happy.

Tell the truth, Bill, I wasn't exactly sure what he was talking about.

He thought you were, that's the important part, right?

I guess he just needed somebody to talk to.

Hey, we talk to him. It's him that's not supposed to talk.

What do you mean?

Not good for him, hasn't got the wind. You didn't notice? Fucker can't breathe.

Asthma?

The other one. Can't be out more than an hour, he's gotta get back to his trailer, got this apparatus in there. Oxygen.

Emphysema?

Borrego gave him a sharp two-fingered salute. Zackary waited for the next thing, but Borrego just stared at him. It was Zackary's turn.

What about his dog?

He's dead.

Yeah, that's what he said.

Let me tell you something, Mr. Ray; a guy like that, don't be surprised one night he goes out, sets fire to one of them colleges he got fired from. Settle the score. I wouldn't be surprised it was him that killed his dog.

Why would he do that?

Like I said.

Dogs get old and die, Bill.

Right. And sometimes they get ground glass.

Borrego being funny, and it was. Zackary grinned.

Inspired, Borrego leaned closer, nailing him with his hooded brown eyes, started snapping his fingers, jackhammering the floor with his foot, slapping the table with his other hand, setting the beat for what was about to come. It came in a gravelly deep voice—Johnny Cash, but tuneless as an auctioneer and just as fast.

You come to a place like this you don't have a clue meet a guy like me you wonder how its gonna be the boys at the bar starting to pout how in the hell is this gonna work out and smarty-pants Fingley you're so worried about waiting in his trailer for his lungs to give out you hunt with the buzzards and run with the hounds sneaking through the desert like a dickheaded clown then caught in the lot like a dirty little wimp but really what it is is a *Photoplay* chimp looking for a cantaloupe so don't tell the tiger she can't eat the antelope . . .

Then he was on his feet, fluttering one hand over his head, marching in place, accelerating the words.

You swam and you sneezed you got down on your knees and what did you think they wouldn't make a stink. Everybody right everybody wrong that's the truth in this little song one thing sure and the rest is lies if you don't smell sweet you won't get the meat won't get to eat Arvid Toby's pretty little sweet I'm slapping my hand stabbing my heal I stiffen I sag I'm giving you chills the Good Book don't say we once had gills but whatever it is we bark and we squeal and steal the pies unzip your fly with fire in the eye in the back of your car where the movies lie . . .

Not missing a beat, he sat back down and went on. And on.

The boys at the bar couldn't watch. They'd seen it before, but this time *the old girl* (that's what they called him behind his back) was outdoing himself, taking it to extremes. Bob, the barman, had disappeared, gone into a back room to get away.

Whatever it was, it would be talked about—a Snake Pit scandal.

Zackary tried to stay detached; it wasn't easy. The rapid pork of Borrego's self-regard embarrassed him, and a part of him was afraid Borrego knew it, knew what he was really thinking. But also he was captivated and paid better than just courteous attention, especially when the doggerel degenerated into gibberish, into an alien language, and he got the sense Borrego's performance was an act of defiance aimed at the absence of a larger clarity. But the last line was shouted distinctly in English, right into his ear.

Blow out your eardrums with a bledsoe horn Movie Man!

This made Zackary laugh, and that was that. The song was sung. Borrego finished what was left in his glass and said:

Drive me home, please.

Relief all around. Zackary tried to pay for the whiskey, but Borrego wouldn't have it. It's taken care of, he said. They went out into the heat, got in the Buick.

Driving south. No moon, a million stars, but not enough to give the desert any help. It was black except for the cataract of road in the headlights. Zackary was looking at that. Borrego was looking at him.

You know why they don't have any pyramids in Tennessee?

Zackary didn't have an answer and hoped Borrego wasn't starting up again.

Because Christians, even if you whip 'em, wouldn't've hauled all that limestone. Right?

The man was drunk, if not insane. Zackary pictured himself about to die and there was nothing he could do about it. Dumped in the desert with a bullet in his head. This was the road to Mexico. And it didn't have any houses on it.

How much farther to your place, Bill?

We're just driving.

Borrego had a big throat, and it took a while to clear it. He did it for about a mile before he spoke again.

Those boys would of kicked your ass if I hadn't of stepped in.

That went without saying, so Zackary didn't say anything. Borrego did.

What about "recursive"?

Recursive what?

Reed. Heard him say it—didn't say it today, but . . . what's it mean?

I'm not sure, Bill, depends how it's used.

Swear words?

No, probably meant it in some kind of mathematical way. About repeating something.

Those boys would have kicked your ass really bad if I hadn't of showed up.

I used to box a bit, but probably you're right, they would of kicked my ass.

Believe it!

I do.

You think I wanna suck your cock?

What?

Zackary tried to laugh. Borrego didn't. He was waiting for a better answer.

No! Why would I think that?

Never entered your mind?

No!

The screech of his own voice shocked him, and he didn't hear what Borrego just said.

What?

I said turn it around! I wanna go back.

A little part of him was almost hurt, but Zackary was thrilled to hear it. He slowed down fast, then, careful not to go off the road and be trapped in the sand, he turned the Buick around.

They didn't look at each other and nobody said a thing. Borrego chewed on his thumb; he had a hangnail, or acted like he did. Zackary tried not to drive over eighty. He couldn't wait to be alone again. After he dropped Borrego off, he'd leave what he left at the Firefly and go straight through the night back to Brentwood, a free man.

They pulled up in front of the Snake Pit and Borrego got out, didn't say a thing. Zackary watched him walk to the front door. It was locked. He pulled a key out of his pants, opened the door, and went in.

S omething woke him up. A vibration. Zackary didn't know what it was. Or where he was. Then he did. It was thunder. He was in the Buick in front of the Snake Pit. It was raining. His shoulder was wet. He rolled up the window. The storm had come down from the mountains, was moving east. In a minute it was gone. He lit a cigarette, rolled down the window.

He drove a block to the China Diner, slowed, but didn't stop. No reason to; it was closed. Not just for the night. He went straight, turned right. Nothing. Made a U-turn, drove another couple blocks, and saw it. The El Dorado trailer park. He would say he had come to get that manual on histograms, the martini too. He was sure Reed Fingley wouldn't be there. Zackary was three years late.

A line from a play he saw when he was in high school came to him. A line he sometimes remembered and liked to say. It was a fiery lawyer, a Clarence Darrow type, said it defending the life of his innocent client, a quote from William Penn: "They have a right to censure that have a heart to help. The rest is cruelty, not justice."

Zackary whispered it, then rapped again on the aluminum door. And waited.

Jean was her name! Suddenly it came to him. The waitress's name was Jean. Married to Arvid Toby by now, if he wasn't killed in Vietnam. By this time probably she'd seen Zackary in a rerun and has had sad, dreamy thoughts of having been kissed by a movie star. In her excitement she must've shared it with somebody. How could she not? Her sister maybe.

But Reed? Nobody answered. The trailer was empty. Zackary looked around at the dripping yard.

A lemon tree, Reed had said, but Zackary didn't see any lemon tree. Either it died or had been cut down. Royal Gallant was supposed to be buried under it. If so, there wouldn't be much left of him, maybe a little fur, some teeth, and the bones.

THE SHAPE
OF THE
FINAL DOG

Kard had a good mind for what he did, but certain words were lost to him, words he heard but couldn't say. Like *breakfast*, couldn't put the sound and the concept together, not that he needed to, he never ate in the morning. Kard was not temperamental and had a high tolerance for pain, soft-spoken and nice to look at, basically obliging, but he had his limits. His small, perfect ears, for instance, were so sensitive, loud noises could unsettle him and trigger violence.

He knew three jokes but never had occasion to tell them. They were in the manual under tactics. About a dog who did something funny with its tail. About a Greek who was hit on the head by a tortoise dropped by an eagle. About something that ended with "Frog legs are funny, but not in a frying pan." And a fourth about a short man who had knowledge of small creatures made of tar, kept them in a drawer and kissed them every night before he went to bed. Kard liked that one, but hadn't memorized it yet. Machines with genes, technical things he understood.

In the waiting room, waiting for his appointment

with Inspector Queen, Kard heard a noise down the hall he did not understand. He knew how to get through doors that were locked, and he did. What he found in the otherwise empty room was a chair facing an eighteen-inch speaker. Above it, there was a photo of a duck. Every ten seconds there was the sound of a quack. He listened awhile, then turned to see who was standing behind him.

This is an off-limits area, Queen said, but I'm proud of you for getting in. He told Kard he could listen another twenty minutes, then come down to his office for instructions and maybe a chat. Against the grain like a saw is how Queen usually went, but not with Kard. A soft spot is what he had; Kard was his favorite tracker.

Kard was competent and young, but not really driven, not yet, that would come in time. Also he had a crooked smile. It looked cordial, but he didn't mean it. It just happened, it was a tic.

Between cell fate manipulation and the zygote activators it got confusing, and Kard needed monitoring on occasion. Nothing was his; all he had was his job, and he wasn't always convinced he had that. Queen had said that being unconvinced was the backbone of it all. Life was a blood race of love against envy. Kard had no idea what that meant. He didn't have the capacity to be baffled, and he never had a friend. For that matter, neither had Queen. But sometimes Kard was curious and sometimes Queen shook his hand for this.

If the cause you serve isn't better than you are, you got the wrong job, Queen told him. That was a slogan that made sense. Another one they liked was, Survival of the fittest means destruction of the duds. Killing dupes keeps you from becoming one. Remember that. Kard did. He was pretty sure that it made no difference where one person ended and another began. His mind was as tight and flat as a prisoner's bed.

Give yourselves up, Steelheads, was a proclamation that hadn't worked. They were stubborn and would rather hide or die than be dismantled. In this case the *dupe* (department slang for *duplicant,* i.e., steelhead) was PFC Sapper Morton, a deserter who had been spotted working in a potato field southwest of Winnipeg.

Inspector Queen sat at his desk with his midday meal, a bowl of rice and mock snails he ate with Chinese eating sticks, and said, It's this chink mush until my new stomach comes in. Then he clarified the details of the assignment until Kard had absorbed them. A Sergeant Falling Horse of the Royal Mounted would meet him at the border and fly him in.

Kard had to go home and get ready for the trip, but Queen kept him a little longer, so they could chat. It was straight from the manual, the idea being to encourage not making mistakes in the future by recalling ones made in the past. A mistake Kard had made with an old man who owned a snake, for instance.

Do you remember a plank house sunk to its windows in sand?

Kard remembered it.

The old man who lived there?

Kard remembered the old man. He had been living there alone a long time.

Under the picture of a dog on the wall what did he have?

Kard remembered a seven-foot rattlesnake in a cage and near it a broken-down piano he didn't know if the old man could play.

Steelheads sometimes offered him food. Kard took their jaws, but not the soup—it felt wrong somehow. But not this time. The old man offered him nothing.

And no dupe he ever interviewed kept a snake.

What? Watch this! The old man screamed.

And, to show Kard his power, stuck his hand in the cage. The snake coiled and buzzed, then it bit him. The old man yanked his arm out and howled. Then fell down and couldn't breathe.

But Kard's mistakes were few, and well within the margins of error, plus he was a good listener, an ear in the museum of Queen's ideas. In a squad meeting once Queen announced, This is my boy! And put his arm around Kard. That was something Kard would never forget.

You looked at the snake awhile, then you left, Queen said.

I was pretty sure a snake couldn't kill a steelhead.

So the old man was just an old man and you didn't have to report it? What else don't you report?

Queen waited, but Kard didn't say.

What about the little blind lady you tried to sell a hamster to? She said she was afraid to touch it and asked you to describe it please. His name is Chunks, you said, and he's got a short tail. He won't bite. Go ahead, he likes you.

He does?

You thought you made her believe it. He's clean, you said. Sleeps all day and very nice at night. He likes to hide. He comes with a box. Touch him.

A soft animal is hard to find, she said. Then, with a bony finger, she touched it. There was a spark. The blind lady bristled. You went for your weapon, a Fermium Six I think it was, but even blind, she was quick and almost got you.

More or less, that's what Kard had said in the report. It was a good report. He didn't hold back.

He never told Queen about Shee. He didn't have to, Queen already knew, but it was good policy to let Kard have one—a secret. So Queen never pressed it. He went back to the subject.

Information on Sapper Morton had come south from a man called Hinge. The following day Kard would go north to act on it. That was it for the chat.

In the bigger picture, hybridized steelheads would be the next step, but before composites of the new model could achieve nexus, the old ones had to be destroyed. For the most part, they were not a problem, but the ones who ran away were more complex. If the dead were still pretty, you killed the right one. *Pretty* was department slang for *posthumously unchanged.* Kard had never asked why.

At home Kard dreamed he found a silver dog whistle buried in the ground. The ground was hard and white, like snow. He blew the whistle as hard as he could, but there was no sound, it summoned nothing.

On nights when he couldn't sleep, he looked at himself in the mirror. Or took a walk. Once he was followed by a man who wanted something and pawed at him, yelled at him. Kard beat the man badly, almost to death. But there was no consolation to it. He got that from Queen. Also from Shee.

Shee was the most beautiful person he had ever seen, but he was never sure that he had seen her. He could feel her, he could hear her. He could tell her he didn't have much to tell, and it felt good—Shee was the mystery of his comfort. But less so lately; it was changing.

Nobody finds anything they don't already know, is what Shee said. And sometimes told him what would happen next. And sometimes it did. Like a brick through the window of himself. But it was changing.

And there were ideas he had that he couldn't explain. Even the old ideas. His clothes, for instance. Not that he didn't like them, he didn't care. From time to time he was told to improve his appearance, get a new suit or have the old one cleaned. Why? His access to privilege was so marginal. Shee tried to help him with these things, and a part of him was tempted to tell her you're either the product of a mother or just a product—instead he told her she was a woman. How did he know?

You were made from one.

I was made of many things.

He would tell her he knew what she looked like.

Is it the picture you carry in your mind?

He would show her the picture in his mind.

Shee would tell him stories about himself, and inspired him to think of how it could be. It took bringing her to mind sincerely, but it had begun to hurt and he didn't want to do it anymore. Kard was changing.

Queen knew about this, the little ups and the downs, and so far, all was fine. Kard had been tested and came out verified every time. But there was always a next time, of not being sure.

If the dead were still pretty, you killed the right one.

There was a number tattooed on the underside of his biceps. Kard had looked it up, but the number meant so many things the information confused him.

He went to Queen, who told him to take off his shirt so he could look. For one thing it's the birth year of Alexander the Great, Queen had said, but that's not what it means. He said that 323 was a gene from the *Homo sapiens* family B. A protein code that contained two phosphotyrosine-binding domains that functioned in accord with signal transduction. Then he laughed and told Kard to put his shirt back on.

Kard packed up his Evaluator and his short-barreled Fermium. The Evaluator weighed just over a pound, six dials, a screen, and a switch. It fit like a snail in the shell of his briefcase. Except for his weapon and the manual, that's all he carried. First the evaluation, then the kill.

Up U.S. 52 to Dugway, North Dakota, just short of the Canadian border, in a rental. He had trawled for runaway steelheads in the boonies before, but never so far north. It was a novelty to his skin.

Things closed up when the sun went down, so Kard spent the night in the car. The melt and blur of simple subjects, like cups on a shelf—it was easy sitting still. When the morning came back, he moved.

A sanatorium called Agnew is where he located Hinge. It was crummy and cold, not a good place to talk, so Kard got a day pass and took him to lunch.

At the cafeteria, Hinge, who was Dutch and good with a pen, traced out an aerial view of a tiny shack and a tractor on a long furrowed field he drew on a napkin. Kard put it in his pocket. Then Hinge's daughter came in. Doris was fat and wanted to eat.

She told Kard a barbecue story. Hinge had given her a cookout to celebrate her sixteenth and caught himself on fire grilling a fish. It felt like an old father-and-daughter routine, both of them grinning waiting for Kard to ask the next question. Kard asked, Who put him out? He asked Hinge, Who put you out?

Nobody! cried Hinge, because Doris and her mom couldn't stop laughing. Hinge laughed harder than Doris, and pulled up his shirt to show Kard the scars.

When they were done eating, Doris went somewhere to shop and Kard took Hinge back to Agnew.

Kard crossed the border for his rendezvous with Sergeant Falling Horse at the North-West Mounted Police Department. There were some papers they showed him that he didn't have to sign, because it was already done. Kard gave Falling Horse the napkin and got in his truck; then they drove to the field.

Falling Horse wore the blue tunic, but not the hat; his hair was black as a brush. He was large, but wore the boots of a child. Kard saw the bottle of raspberry vodka he kept under the seat.

Kard didn't think Indians were supposed to talk very much, but Falling Horse never stopped. Even talked about the trees they passed on the road.

Each of them trees is worth two hundred dollars, he shouted. When you see a lot of trees like this it means there's plenty of water. Some say, Bullshit, there's no water, not in a hundred miles of here! But they'd be dead wrong. You see those bitches going up the road back there?

Kard had not.

Whole gang of 'em. They run together!

You mean girls?

No! Dogs! Real ones.

Kard didn't believe it. Falling Horse wasn't making sense, he talked to make noise.

I was eighteen months overseas. I don't go talking

about it except with people who been there. You been there?

No.

And they can tell if I'm lying too.

Why would they think you were lying?

Because this was back in the war. Back when all the blues came from Toronto. I could play single string with the best of 'em. I need to stop at a store.

They did stop. Kard stayed in the car, and an hour later they were in the air.

There was a wind-shear condition, but it didn't bother Falling Horse; he knew what he was doing even though he couldn't get the heater to work. He asked Kard if he could fly, just in case something went wrong—Falling Horse was a joker.

What if I have a heart attack?

Kard did know how to fly, but didn't say anything.

As they got higher the pitch of the turbo got thinner, sounded like a motorbike, and it got colder. Falling Horse once in a while had a glance at the napkin to make sure to get where they were going. And in less than an hour they did.

Cold, somber terrain plowed and planted for potatoes, miles of it. A tractor down there rising and falling over the furrows. At twelve feet off the ground, a little black dog appeared and gave chase. Falling Horse hovered the spinner, then softly, in a puff of dust, touched down. The dog had a bad front leg, stiff as a stick. Yapping and snapping, but keeping a distance, it circled the spinner. The hatch slid open and Kard climbed out.

Ten years ago the whole area was forest, but people couldn't eat trees, so now it's potatoes, is what Horse said. Kard told him to stay in the spinner, keep an eye on things, and walked away. Horse drank what was left of the vodka and fell asleep.

On his way to the cabin, Kard stopped to look at the dog. It was pointy-eared and watchful. It stared back for a few moments, then turned away, sat down in the dirt to watch the fields. He waited for it to turn again and look at him. It didn't.

Sixty-seven klicks out of Akutan on the southern slopes of the Laurentian Shield is where they were. How Sapper Morton got here was a question Inspector Queen would want an answer to.

Within one potato there are mountains and rivers.

Recovered steelheads were worthless, but for the public good they could not be left to roam. Separated they had no cohesion, they drifted and hid.

All he needed was Sapper's jaw. Nothing to take but that. That was the job. And he could take the dog too if he wanted. There was enough space in the spinner for that. The daylight weak, but Kard could see the tractor out there rising and falling over the furrows, one headlight piercing the speckled air. The plowman wore goggles and a dust mask. But Kard knew who it was.

The front door was at the back porch. He opened it

and went in. One room, one window, one door, walls quilted with old newspapers. A table, a cot, and a chair. There was a pot simmering on the burner next to a pile of potato skins. He removed the Evaluator from his briefcase—six dials, a screen, and a switch.

Always a piano. An upright, scratched and chipped, yellowing keys. A steelhead could lift one in a snap. It was here because Sapper must have carried it. But could he play it? That was a question Kard had never yet asked.

And there was a photo pinned to the wall, Kard had seen it before. Steelheads with pictures of themselves— it was what was left of their pride. All of them had been in the army. No one knew why. The ones who got out and took off always had pianos. But Sapper was the first Kard ever saw with a dog. Both had brown eyes.

Kard's eyes were on the piano keys; he never played one himself, not so much as a note. Then he heard footsteps heavy on the porch, saw the plowman pass the window. The floorboards at the door sagged under the weight of him as he came in.

Sapper was long and strong, unhealthy-looking skin, blotchy, shoulders stooped, eyes sunken, knobby cheek-bones. He closed the door, then turned to face Kard, but not directly. Kard's voice was gentle, unsurprised.

Where is your dog, Mr. Morton?

Sapper was shy; it took a few moments to get his words to come.

Outside. Who are you?

I'm from the CPA, Mr. Morton. The Canadian Potato Association.

Pulling himself to attention, Sapper recited the Canadian Potato Association motto:

"Within one potato there are mountains and rivers."

Kard was impressed. Sapper was either trickier or more evolved than he looked.

That was good. Do you have a name for your dog?

No.

Shall I tell you why I'm here?

Yes.

I'm to do a survey on tenant farmers to see if growth ratio and land allotments are keeping pace with each other. Do you understand?

Sapper dimly nodded, then looked at the Evaluator blinking and purring on the table. Then he looked away, to the soup on the stove, boiling low and steady.

What's that you're cooking there? It smells pretty good.

Sapper went to the burner, checked the pot, then turned to look at Kard. His eyes doggish and sad, hopeful maybe.

Do you want some?

That would be nice. Thank you.

It took time for him to get the bowl. Kard watched him pour soup into it. Carefully, Sapper brought it to the table, with a spoon. There was only the one chair; he stepped aside and waited for Kard to sit on it.

Before I try the soup, Sapper, I want you to sit on the

chair. I need to ask you some questions. Will you do that?

I already had my dinner.

Before I have mine, I need you to sit down.

Sapper started to, but hesitated. It was the Evaluator that troubled him.

Do I have to?

You don't have to, but it won't take long. All you have to do is sit down and be very still. Can you do that?

Slowly, as if afraid the weight of him might break the chair, Sapper sat down. Duplicants were disadvantaged from beginning to end, but never knew it. Kard knew it, and it divided him, it made him tired, but he forced himself to pay attention.

Now please, put your hand on the table.

Sapper lifted his hand. His fingers were short and strong, nails like burnt rubber. His hand trembled above the table.

Go ahead, Sapper, it'll be fine, lay it down on the table.

Either Sapper couldn't or he wouldn't. He looked up, one eye twitching, a plea in his gravelly voice.

I took this test before, I think.

Kard preferred to keep the questions in order. *How did you get here? Did anyone help you? Do you play the piano?* But it was too late for that. The pulsing of the Evaluator had increased. Kard knew what was coming next, and for the sake of his ears stepped back.

Nobody ever sees me!

That's not true, Sapper. If it was, I wouldn't be here.

Sapper got louder.

I work with objects, not people—I drive the tractor!

There was no room in the spinner for Sapper, but Kard made the offer—it was in the manual.

Why don't we just leave, and you come back to the city with me?

Sapper had turned dark, indignant. Kard shrugged as Sapper stumbled to his feet, brought his fist down on the table like a hammer. Kard snatched the Evaluator off the table as it collapsed, set it on the counter and turned.

He released the safety on his Fermium and shot Sapper three times, twice in the chest and once in the groin. Sapper went down so hard he cracked the floor. His stout legs buckled under him, no blood, but he was dead.

Kard had four minutes before the cabin contaminated. He bent down, pinched Sapper's cheek. The skin stayed puckered like putty. Kard pulled open the mouth, inserted two fingers, and tugged the jaw loose. He held it up, squinting at the ID. According to the law, nonpersons, animals, and plants had no rights and were regarded as property. Sapper was the product of Culvert Industries.

Kard went to the sink, washed his hands, then turned off the burner. The half-life of a moderated Fermium round was less than a day—the place would be normal tomorrow.

The sun was gone, the land had darkened, but the air still had some light. The dog had moved again; now it was standing by the tractor. As Kard approached, it slinked away.

Sapper had left his goggles and dust mask on the seat; the onboard radio was broadcasting farm bureau weather reports. Kard turned it off and followed the dog back towards the spinner. As he came closer, the dog started to bark and backed away, afraid to run and afraid to stay.

Come on, come on, Jib.

He called it Jib and didn't know why, and whispering, he came closer:

You're gonna be all alone . . . come on, come on . . . I'll take you home.

There was room in the spinner for the dog, on his lap. Kard was about to grab him when suddenly the dog froze and fell over, legs stiff, jaw clamped shut; but the barking continued. For a few moments Kard listened as the sound weakened. He should have known better.

Falling Horse was awake and watching. He wanted to say something, but there was nothing to say. Kard climbed in. The hatch slid shut, the turbo revved, and in a whirl of dust, the spinner lifted into the shrouded sky.

END

ACKNOWLEDGMENTS

To Bryony Atkinson, who started it, and for Racquel Palmese, whom I could do nothing without, and Jason Patric, who opened the door. For the abiding help of Rosalie and Noah Kaplan, Elizabeth Rubin, Jessica Kerwin Jenkins, Lew McCreary, Mary Beth Hughes. To David Rosenthal for offering the chance. And Sarah Hochman for everything. Thank you.

ABOUT THE AUTHOR

Hampton Fancher is an author and screenwriter. His writing credits include *Blade Runner* and *The Mighty Quinn*, and he is the writer and director of *The Minus Man* (winner of the Grand Prix Jury Award, Montreal World Film Festival). He began his career as a flamenco dancer in Europe and has acted in numerous films and television shows. He has taught acting classes in Los Angeles and screenwriting at Columbia and New York Universities. Born in East Los Angeles, he lives in Brooklyn, New York. This is his first work of fiction.